EXTRAORDINARY RENDITIONS

Extraordinary Renditions

Andrew Ervin

BROOKLYN
BOOK FESTIVAL
9/12/10

COFFEE HOUSE PRESS
MINNEAPOLIS 2010

COVER AND BOOK DESIGN by Linda Koutsky
AUTHOR PHOTO © Eddy Perez

Coffee House Press books are available to the trade through our primary distributor, Consortium Book Sales & Distribution, www.cbsd.com or (800) 283-3572. For personal orders, catalogs, or other information, write to: info@coffeehousepress.org.

Coffee House Press is a nonprofit literary publishing house. Support from private foundations, corporate giving programs, government programs, and generous individuals helps make the publication of our books possible. We gratefully acknowledge their support in detail in the back of this book.

To you and our many readers around the world,
we send our thanks for your continuing support.

LIBRARY OF CONGRESS CIP INFORMATION
Ervin, Andrew.
Extraordinary renditions / Andrew Ervin.
p. cm.
ISBN 978-1-56689-246-9 (alk. paper)
1. Composers—Fiction. 2. Soldiers—Fiction.
3. Women musicians—Fiction. 4. Budapest (Hungary)—Fiction. I. Title.
PS3605.R855E98 2010
813'.6—DC22 ISBN
2010016173

PRINTED IN CANADA
1 3 5 7 9 8 6 4 2
FIRST EDITION | FIRST PRINTING

ACKNOWLEDGMENTS
Special thanks to my parents and to the entire Ervin, Pierrou, and Varga families; Chris Abani, Setareh Atabeigi, Christian Bauman, Madison Smartt Bell, Jane Bennett, Derek Chafin, Clay Cook, Ricardo Cortez Cruz, Julia Glass, Michael Harrison, Troy Hendricks, Tayari Jones, Laurie Kaplan, Tamás Kovács, Nikki Larsen, Noah Larsen, J. Robert Lennon, Bayo Ojikutu, Stewart O'Nan, Steph Opitz, Audrey Petty, Richard Powers, Alice Randall, Tim Reeder, Kevin Richards, Amy Sayre-Roberts, Jodee Stanley, Charles Sullivan, William T. Vollmann, and Curtis White; Chris Fischbach, Anitra Budd, Molly Mikolowski, Esther Porter, and everyone at Coffee House Press; Ira Silverberg at Sterling Lord Literistic; MIT Press for permission to quote from Anna Bostock's translation of *The Theory of the Novel,* by György Lukács; and Tariq "Black Thought" Trotter of the Roots for permission to quote from "I Will Not Apologize." Excerpts from this book appeared in *Conjunctions* and *The Southern Review.*

To Elivi

I recall a conversation with Frau Marianne Weber in the late autumn of 1914. She wanted to challenge my attitude by telling me of individual, concrete acts of heroism. My only reply was: "The better the worse!" When I tried at this time to put my emotional attitude into conscious terms, I arrived at more or less the following formulation: the Central Powers would probably defeat Russia; this might lead to the downfall of Tsarism; I had no objection to that. There was also some probability that the West would defeat Germany; if this led to the downfall of the Hohenzollerns and the Hapsburgs, I was once again in favour. But then the question arose: who was to save us from Western civilisation?

—GYÖRGY LUKÁCS,
PREFACE TO *The Theory of the Novel* (1962)

14 Bagatelles

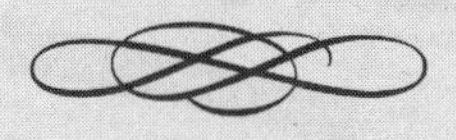

14 BAGATELLES

I.

The cab ride from the airport was more exhausting than the transoceanic flight. Budapest had grown unrecognizable, and filthy. Everything had changed. Only the weather was familiar now—the dry cold and the wind that rushed down along the river, sustained by clogged and muddy streets. Harkályi felt grateful for the generic familiarity of the hotel room, the bland tones of the wallpaper. With the curtains drawn, he remained placeless a while longer, a measure closer to anonymity, yet something was different this time. They called him Hungarian, but that was a designation he never felt. Perhaps he should not have come.

The last time Harkályi had been in Hungary was when, four decades earlier, he received word of the failing health of Zoltán Kodály, his old friend and mentor. They had spoken in pidgin Hungarian of history and progress, of the varieties of immortality. "This wax," Kodály admonished him, holding aloft the sleeve containing a newly pressed edition of his *Székely fonó,* "is nothing less than a gravestone for my music."

There is eternal life, Kodály had said, not afforded by so many of these sonically miraculous recordings, but bestowed upon a teacher by his most loyal student.

Harkályi had since grown old. His face in the washroom mirror had become significantly looser since his last visit. His hair was once brown, his eyesight as perfect as his precisely tuned inner ear. He had come here again, ostensibly, to witness the premiere of his opera *The Golden Lotus.* There were other reasons, reasons he did not yet dwell upon.

Sitting on the edge of the bed, he unlaced his shoes and waited for his luggage to be brought up. He removed five thousand forints for a gratuity from his billfold and put it on the bedside table. The telephone receiver was heavy, leaden. The light on the base flashed at him until he pressed a series of buttons. The first message, in broken English, came from an orchestra representative: they will send a car to the hotel tomorrow in the early afternoon, and then ferry him to the concert over in Buda, where he will meet the prime minister. "Szank you," the voice concluded, "and velcome home."

After the performance, the prime minister will personally bestow upon Harkályi a medal in recognition of his contribution to the artistic legacy of the nation and service to the Hungarian people. Tomorrow's event will represent the final public engagement of his career, his crowning achievement. Afterwards, he will return to his university residency in Philadelphia and remove himself, once again, from public view, taking on only a precious few students of significant artistic promise. He was ready to stop moving, finally, to stop becoming.

Since the death of Kodály, even newer and seemingly more miraculous recording technologies had emerged, hissing and popping from the primordial carbon ooze, only to find themselves soon surpassed in aural verisimilitude and returned to oblivion, extinct. Digital reproduction promised nothing less than an end to entropic degradation. Millions of people had by now bought compact discs containing a rendition of Harkályi's Symphony No. 4 as arranged for a unique and all-but-infinite string of 1s and 0s. His was the first small-C classical recording to alchemize from plastic to gold, and then from gold to platinum, and to depose a savvily angry hip-hop performer, however briefly, from atop the pop-music charts: millions of plastic mirrors, simulacra of simulacra extending so far that the original, an outdoor performance in Jerusalem a decade ago, could no longer be heard.

Even those compact discs were nearly obsolete now—just as Kodály had predicted. Fraunhofer-Gesellschaft's inventive Moving Picture Expert Group Audio Layer III technology offered Harkályi's music the portable convenience of unimaginable compression, of innumerable notes and rests packed together, traveling shoulder to shoulder through the ether and into the headphones of young people who consumed it the way they consumed meat, incognizant of the slaughter it entailed. Easy, infinite reproduction made him a millionaire, a real millionaire, but at the risk of thoughtless and carefree disposability.

The second message was from his niece, Magda, who will accompany him to the concert. He hadn't seen her in nearly two years, since she finished her graduate studies at Yale and accepted a position as an interpreter with a consulting firm based in Washington, DC. Presently working at a military base in southern Hungary, among other places, much of what she did was classified even from him. He will meet her in the hotel's famous pastry shop at eleven in the morning. As his only remaining blood relative, Magda was the sole heir to the inexplicably enormous fortune his recordings had earned him, though a number of charitable institutions also stood to benefit from what he imagined to be a pending and not entirely unwelcome demise. It will be lovely to see her, a warm relief from the strain and headache of travel and public appearance, the weight of long-deferred nostalgia. He replaced the phone on its cradle and the red light died out at once.

He remained seated on the bed, holding back the memories he resisted all of these years and had some reason to fear. He surrendered and accepted the standing invitation of the Hungarian government. It was time to address the dybbuks he had avoided for so long; so he returned to the Hungarian soil to seek forgiveness, as he had once sought Kodály's. He came seeking silence. The wrinkled, spotty hands covering his face became damp.

Despite his exhaustion, he knew that he would not sleep; usually, he would be fortunate to gain three hours of rest. It was at night that he saw the emaciated faces reflected back at him as if from the hundreds of thousands of compact discs he had set loose upon the world. What took you so long to return? That would be the first question they asked. They will speak to him in Czech and Polish and Hebrew and Romany and Hungarian, languages he understood fluently in the twilight of semiconsciousness, but in which he could never answer. His first language was that of notation, of music, but none of his compositions to date appeased the faces as they did the many satisfied customers and concertgoers worldwide.

He stood with an inaudible groan and wandered through the suite turning down all of the heaters. The sitting room offered a view of the monolithic building opposite the hotel and of the traffic below on the Szent István körút. It was only midafternoon, yet it already grew dark. There was much to do. A yellow tram glided past, down the center of the road, toward the river. Overall-clad workmen on ladders struggled to hang flags from the lampposts in anticipation of the holiday. They were difficult to attach in the harsh wind, which Harkályi could not feel from the comfort of his room. The men argued and laughed. They passed around a plastic cola bottle half-full of pale wine. A knock came at the door and he took the forints from the table, folded the bill in his palm. A young porter stood next to an elaborate, brass handcart. "Harkályi Lajos?"

"Igen." Yes.

"Beszél magyarul?"

"Well, no. I am afraid that I do not."

He stepped aside and the porter wheeled the squeaking trolley into the room. It contained just one suitcase and one hanging suit bag. The porter looked at him. He was twenty or twenty-five years old and attired in the formal finery of the hotel trade, the tailed coat smelling of car exhaust and cigarette smoke. The porter stared for a moment. "You are the composer," he said.

"Yes."

"My girlfriend, she has your CD."

"Oh. Well, please give her my regards." He considered withholding the money.

"She doesn't listen to it very much because it makes her cry."

How was he to respond? The hotel clothes didn't fit the boy especially well, and he had neglected to shave for several days; his teeth were not very well cared for. "Thank you," Harkályi said, and handed him the forints, which the porter, without acknowledgment, slipped into a pocket of his untailored red pants. He then deposited the suitcase onto the room's luggage rack and hung the suit bag inside the armoire. Harkályi remained standing at the door, holding it open. The hallway was empty, free of people and hideously carpeted. He opened the door wider, but the porter did not retreat right away.

"I am Miklós," the boy said. "Press the concierge button on your telephone if you need anything. Ask for Miklós." He lifted his round hat a centimeter above his head for an instant and pulled the cart behind himself, back into the hallway.

"I will do just that very thing, Miklós—thank you."

"Anything at all," he said. "I—" But Harkályi closed the door.

He started to unpack. It would be a short stay, less than forty-eight hours, so he had not brought much. In his suitcase, on top, he found a foreign, white document from the United States authorities alerting him to the fact that they had randomly searched his bag for purposes of national security. His clothes and belongings appeared unmolested, however, and he placed them in neat piles into drawers. He had carried with him a second, nicer pair of shoes and, for Magda, some chocolates and an advance copy of his newest recording, his Concerto for Violin as performed by a technically flawless and altogether unmusical young star and the Cleveland Orchestra.

He had left his briefcase in the bedroom. From it he drew his leather shaving kit and a small, mostly round stone. It was the size of a baby's fist and tears and years of wear had buffed it smooth; it had traveled with him for longer than he wanted to remember. He planned to leave it in Hungary, where it was given to him. He put it on the bedside table, taking care that it did not scratch the glass surface.

He needed a nap, but sleep would not take him. Too weary to yet venture outside, he stared for hours, utterly motionless, at the carnage transmitted to the suite's television set. It was like an open sewer line spilling onto the carpet. He had seen it all already, yet the circularity of history did not bring him comfort. When he felt the grumbling of his stomach, Harkályi slipped back into his more comfortable shoes, his overcoat, and his hat and gloves. He carried the stone in an outer pocket of his jacket. Opening his billfold, he confirmed the presence of his key card and stepped out into the hallway, pulling the door tight behind him.

There were others waiting for the elevator, a woman and two children. They spoke low German, a familiar dialect of his first language. They were going downstairs, to the pastry shop, for cakes. "Cukrászda"—that was one of those words, one of the few he remembered from childhood, for which there was no exact or effective English equivalent. "Ideges" was another. When the elevator arrived, the older of the girls demanded the privilege of pressing the L button while the other got to press CLOSE. They squealed and wiggled like two already-overfed Teutonic hogs. In the metallic reflection of the doors, the four of them looked like a family, a grandfather taking the children out for pizza and ice cream, but the elevator stopped and the image was split in half, down the middle, as a suited businessman entered. He inspected the lighted buttons and, satisfied, hummed a melody that Harkályi to his horror recognized as his own, the main theme of his Symphony No. 4. The piece that made him famous, and wealthy. He made a mental note to take the stairs in the future.

2.

The temperature and fetid air—diesel exhaust, grease, burned meat—attacked him, an all-powerful and immovable force that he knew would shadow him for the next two days. It was already late, and even colder than he had anticipated, colder than his memory allowed, and he worried that his overcoat alone would not keep him warm. A heavier sweater hung in the closet upstairs, but he did not dare risk returning to the room and becoming further waylaid by the same indecision that had kept him away for so many years. He had been cold before; it would not kill him.

Harkályi enjoyed walking, exploring by foot every city he visited, though doing so had become more difficult of late. In the previous decade he visited every medium and large city in Europe, Asia, and North America, forsaking only Budapest, the city from which he had disappeared as a child. Tonight, however, he must first find a restaurant. He had purchased an expensive guidebook, but knew better than to trust the culinary advice contained therein. He had in his travels learned that the book's audience was considerably younger than himself, and he preferred not to subject his ears to the auditory torture of what passed for music in those establishments. As in every city, the trick to finding a suitable place for a meal would involve a willingness to traverse the side streets, to ignore the glossy maps.

The workmen were long gone, presumably to a warm pub. Hungarian flags now flew from all of the lampposts along the ring road, though the wind threatened to shred them into swatches of red, white, and green. People rushed beneath them unaware of all that they possessed by virtue of their belonging here; they pushed past him, smoking cigarettes and speaking over each other, quite noisily, in a language he did not know to his satisfaction. The traffic was marvelous in its density, consistent with that of Berlin or London or Rome, yet seemingly even more aggressive than in those places, competitive. He passed a hair salon that was affixed to the hotel, a bookshop, a butcher with ugly brown sausages hanging in long rows, a steamy pizzeria, a shoe store, another shoe store, a few places the purposes of which he could not determine, closed and darkened. The window of a music shop contained a small display of operatic compact discs. Recordings of Kodály and Erkel and Verdi and Puccini were arranged in a small ziggurat of plastic. Some of his own releases were interspersed throughout. Then it caught his attention: a glossy publicity photograph of himself hung in the window attached to two clear strings that resembled fishing line. It was an advertisement for the concert tomorrow, which, he had been led to believe, had sold out months earlier. They had pasted his photo, crookedly, onto a large sheet of cardboard. In it he was dressed almost exactly as he was now: black overcoat, charcoal-gray turtleneck. His hair in the photo was longer, however, Einsteinian. The image embarrassed him, and he moved along before he could be seen gazing upon his own reflection.

At the end of the block, a wide ramp steered him beneath the körút to an underpass, a colorful expanse with escalators leading down to the subway and steps up to the same trams he had seen from his hotel room. Folk musicians competed with bums for attention and spare change. Men sold telephone cards in front of a bank of blue, unused payphones. Burger King, TourInform, a flower shop, the locked entrance to a massive supermarket. A hallway beyond the escalators led, he remembered, to the rear of the train station. He found it difficult to differentiate the words being spoken around him, the signage. Virág. An old woman, even older than himself, held a baking dish full of tiny, white, bulbous flowers in little leafy bundles, each maybe three inches tall. An elaborate, decorative scarf covered her head. Hóvirág—snow flowers. That was the name. Their appearance heralded the onset of spring, the end of another long winter. Harkályi approached her. "Csókolom," he said. He had at his command the vocabulary of a child.

Her eyes brightened angelically. She appeared genuinely cheerful and merry, despite her degraded condition. Her cheeks revealed the frigidity of the atmosphere, only slightly warmer down here. "Jó estét kivánok."

As a boy, he would with some anxiety await the first hóvirág of the spring, which, in a private ritual, he would wrap in similar bundles and present to his mother. They stayed on the windowsill of the kitchen, in cups of chipped and brightly glazed ceramic, some until the August heat descended from the Mátras, from Slovakia and farther.

"Menny?"

"Tessék?"

He spoke slower, "Menny?"

"Mennyi?"

"Yes—igen. Mennyi?"

"Száz forint."

He didn't have any coins, or even a hundred-forint bill. The automated teller machine at the airport dispensed only five- and ten-thousand forint notes. He offered her five thousand and she shook her head, dismayed. She pointed to the TourInform office, where he could get change, were they open. "No," he said. "All of them. Minden." He waved his gloved hand over the flowers like a benediction and she finally understood. From the bag at her feet she took out a sheet of newspaper from yesterday's *Magyar Hírlap*, and laid it on the filthy concrete floor of the underpass. Harkályi expected to see his own picture looking up at himself again, but it did not appear. The old woman spread out the bundles of flowers on the paper, which soaked up water from the bottom of her baking pan. Lifting it from the corners, she placed the entire bundle in a flimsy plastic bag with vertical yellow stripes, loosely tied the handles together, and held it out for him. "Tessék," she said, and quickly, with a furtive look around, slipped the five thousand forints into a pocket of her peasant skirt. "Nagyon szépen köszönöm," she told him, collected her belongings, and walked quickly to the metro. He was left standing there with a bagful of soggy newspaper—yesterday's news no less—and a garden's worth of quickly dehydrating flowers. He could not help but laugh, and as he did a man of dark complexion, Gypsy maybe, or Turkish, slouched past and whispered, "Change money?" without looking at him.

3.

His glove gripped the conveyor belt, a dirty loop of black rubber leading endlessly into the abyss of the metro station below, circling beneath the iron teeth of the escalator at a greater rate of speed than that of the steps themselves. It moved too rapidly for his comfort, pulling his arm gently down ahead of him. But he did not want to let go; it was an extremely long descent, deep into the core of the city. Of the four long escalators only the outer two were in operation, one moving quickly upward and one downward. Vinyl siding the color of dark wood covered the walls and ceiling of the rounded tunnel and was plastered with stickers and crude illustrations upon which he refused to allow his gaze to linger. A series of plastic-framed advertisements whirred past him faster than he could discern them; a colorful fast-food cup slid down the metal barrier between his and the next escalator over. He watched it descend ahead of him and crash to the station floor. There was laughter at his back.

At the bottom, thrown from the machine, Harkályi was forced to step over the pile of ice cubes and in the process very nearly stumbled, regaining his balance only at the last instant. The bag of flowers fell from his hands and spilled to the ground, mixing with the ice cubes and cola. Four teenagers exited the escalator behind him and stepped on the hóvirág as they passed, smashing them with their boots. They continued past into the darkened corners of the station. Harkályi tried to collect the flowers again but nearly all were crushed. No one stopped to help him gather them from the ground. The old néni who had sold them to him was still waiting for her subway; she turned quickly away out of what appeared to be either embarrassment or disgust. He had no idea what to do with them now. To throw them away would be unthinkable. He left the most flattened of the bunch but returned the remainder to their newspaper-lined bag. They were a delightful burden. Magda would appreciate them.

The Nyugati M3 stop consisted of one long hallway interrupted by a series of metallic pillars. The silver letters above one of the tracks spelled ÚJPEST-KÖZPONT and, above the other, KÖBÁNYA-KISPEST. He was not sure which direction to take, as he did not yet have in mind a specific destination, so he moved toward the sound of the first oncoming train. When it stopped, dozens of people rushed from it, hollering and laughing and passing around bottles of wine and beer. A young woman wearing large headphones stumbled to a stop in front of him. He could not see her eyes through her sunglasses, but the volume of the so-called music emanating from her head was staggering. She looked up at him smilingly, reached into a pocket of her shabby coat, and produced a small safety pin, which, with some difficulty, she attached to the lapel of his overcoat. He made no move to stop her. When she finished he saw that affixed to the pin was a small ribbon of red, white, and green. She smiled and Harkályi watched her walk unsteadily away. She halted at the foot of the upward escalator, went over to the other, downward one, and picked up the remainder of his broken flowers. She gently dusted them off, tried to mend the damaged stems, and carried them in front of her like a bridal bouquet, back up to the city.

The subway left without him, a state of affairs he accepted as an omen to go in the other direction, south, toward Deák Ferenc Square. With the exception of several bums, Harkályi stood alone on the platform. Someone had spray-painted a swastika, of all possible profanities, on the wall map of Budapest, dividing the city into quarters, like Vienna after the war. He could feel the weight of the emptiness in his stomach. It was a strange sensation to be underground here, again, yet not an entirely unwelcome one.

A rush of hot, stale air preceded the sound of the train's arrival. Newspapers and paper bags took flight like so many sickly birds. Pulling to a moderately slow, metallic halt, the sky-blue cars appeared old and not very well tended-to at all. Dirt and colorless geometric graffiti covered the entire side of the train, which cracked open in two places and birthed another mass of red-faced young people into his midst. They jostled past him, taking with them their laughter, which ascended the escalator. As he stepped on board he could see, in the gap between the platform and the floor of the train, something shining amid the oily rocks lining the track bed; he couldn't make out the precise shape before the orange light above his head buzzed and the doors slammed shut, sealed tight and airless by wide, vertical strips of black rubber.

The only other occupants were two teens pressed romantically against the doors at the other end of the car. The train slowed to a stop at, according to the sign posted above the door, ARANY JÁNOS UTCA, named for the father of Hungarian nationalist poetry—some said of Hungarian nationalism itself. There, two Gypsies, one skinny and one preposterously fat, entered through the rear doors. It occurred to him that he had not purchased a ticket. The larger of them looked at Harkályi, but avoided making eye contact. The train started to move. He placed the wet plastic bag on the seat beside him and discretely patted the left side of his breast, as if his billfold may have already disappeared, and shoved his hands deeper into his pockets in order to keep his arms fast against his body for protection. The skinnier of the two men stood at the far door, looking out into the nothingness of subterranean Budapest, while the other planted his sizeable frame strangely close to the groping couple. Harkályi stared at him, watched him slide his right elbow forcefully against the small of the young man's back. The boy did not respond. With his left hand—

Harkályi saw all of this quite clearly—the Gypsy easily removed the boy's wallet from the back pocket of his dungarees, then discretely handed it to the skinny man. The skinny man walked to the front of the train, toward Harkályi, and flashed a defiant smile that convinced him to remain silent. The Gypsies stood in their respective doorways and remained there even as the train stopped at Deák Square, the hub of the entire metro system, where all three of the city's underground lines met. Would-be riders approached the doors of his car from the platform, but seeing the dark-skinned men blocking their paths, moved on quickly to the adjoining cars. When the orange lights buzzed again, signaling that the doors would now close, both men darted out, leaving Harkályi alone once more with the young lovers. He felt for his billfold one more time and found it safely in place. He had trouble controlling his breathing. When he got off at Ferenciek Square he looked back to see that the victimized lovers remained oblivious, ignorant, for the time being, of what had occurred. The hóvirág, which Harkályi had forgotten, traveled with them.

4.

A small cadre of waiters appeared from the kitchen, each burdened by a gigantic, round tray covered with flutes of pale, sparkling wine. They marched out in a solemn, single-file line, followed closely behind by an equal number of young waitresses in traditional, tightly bodiced servant attire. The conversations, the clink-clinking of silver against glass, even the drunken sing-along emanating from another, unseen room, all petered out until the entire coffee house arrived at a briefly sustained moment of silent incredulity. The processional soon splintered off into discrete pairs, who then distributed complimentary beverages to every table.

The building lacked the old-world charm that Harkályi had anticipated, but it was indeed warm and lively and appeared capable of providing an authentic Hungarian meal. He sat on a bench along the right-hand wall of the wide, main room, which also housed two long rows of round tables and a series of close-together, four-man tables, one of which he shared with three tweed-clad and spectacled men engaged in a rigorous debate he couldn't comprehend. He took them for university professors, or some other variety of public intellectual. A balcony opposite his seat contained yet another seating area, and from the sound, there seemed to be even more dining rooms hidden from his current view. He watched the men at his table order coffee after coffee, which they interrupted with the occasional Unicum, an oil-black digestive that smelled uncomfortably like compost and left a green-blue coat inside the bulbs of their stemmed glasses. They didn't acknowledge him. A raucous game of chess two tables over earned a small crowd of observers.

A mustachioed waiter appeared at their table holding over his right shoulder a heavy tray of glassware. The waitress with him carefully plucked four of them from different sections of the tray's surface, helping the waiter maintain a safely balanced distribution of weight. "Tessék," she said, setting one before each of them at the table. The intellectuals did not respond or even appear to notice. "Köszönöm szépen," Harkályi told her, earning a lovely smile despite fumbling so egregiously over his pronunciation and, without question, his accent. The men at his table turned briefly toward the foreigner among them and then promptly resumed their strenuous argument and gesticulation. No one else acknowledged the sparkling wine, so Harkályi ignored his as well, busying himself by consulting his map yet again and watching the excitement around him. The bubbles in his flute soon stopped rising and conspired around the lip of the glass. In the time of his grandparents, and even of his parents, the coffee house had served as the firmament of Budapest's social and intellectual spheres. It was an informal establishment, or less formal than in years past, yet it remained governed by a certain civility that he did appreciate. He had found nothing similar in America, and only distant approximations in Vienna and Paris.

The noise slowly swelled until, at midnight, the maître d'hôtel appeared near his station at the exit and, with a wireless microphone, begged for the attention of his patrons, who obediently complied. The massive team of waiters and waitresses then stood among the tables, each with his or her own glass of formerly sparkling wine. Even a few of the white-clad chefs stood in the kitchen doors for the duration of the five-minute speech, of which Harkályi clearly discerned just "Magyarország" and "szabadság," which the maître d' repeated frequently. Hungary and liberty. It was a toast in honor of Independence Day, the anniversary of the 1848 uprising against the Hapsburg Dynasty—and the outward excuse for Harkályi's return. When he finished, finally, the maître d' lifted his glass, looked around at his attentive audience, and said, "Egészségetekre."

The others at Harkályi's table lifted their glasses. "Egészségedre, egészségedre," they said all at once, and touched their glasses to Harkályi's. "Egészségedre."

He was uncertain, at first, how to respond. "Cheers," he said. "Cheers. Cheers."

One of the intellectuals, the man next to him on the bench, asked him, "You are English?" His thick eyeglasses did not mask the circles beneath his eyes, which were as black as the peels of rotten bananas.

"No. I am . . . I am an American, I guess you could say." He longed for the distraction of his meal, if only the chefs would stay in the kitchen long enough to prepare it.

"American," another of the men said. He was fat and bald, with a face more sympathetic than those of the others. The buttons of his shirt barely contained the body and undershirt trying to escape from beneath them. "We will teach you to say 'egészségedre.' It means—"

"'To your health,'" Harkályi said.

"You can speak Hungarian?"

"No, but I learned a small amount as a child. I was born here in Budapest."

"What? Then you are a Hungarian, not an American!" the third interrogator said. He was only slightly less fat.

"Egészségedre," the man next to him repeated, and they finally sipped their wine, which was cloying, almost unbearable, in its sweetness.

"Why is it that you say you are an American?"

"My family, we spoke German at home—before the war."

Recognition, perhaps even some vague, uncomfortable understanding, passed over them. The first man, the one next to Harkályi, motioned for a passing waiter. "Négy Unicum," he ordered. There was silence for a measure or two. "Where did they send you?"

These were things that Harkályi did not talk about, yet his personal background had become public knowledge, a cultural commodity to be sold and bought and consumed. Despite his reluctance, his embarrassment, and his guilt, his story existed independent of himself; it was as well-known, or known better, than even his music. Some words were not fit to be spoken aloud, yet he invoked them here: "To Terezín."

"You were very young."

"I was fifteen years old when the camps became liberated. My brother and I, we went to America."

"And now you have returned," the fat man said.

"To the scene of the crime," the slightly less fat man said. He was extremely drunk.

"Tessék," the waiter said, and deposited four glasses of Unicum on the table. He also carried with him a small kettle of goulash, which was hung suspended above a tea candle he placed in front of Harkályi. He ladled a portion of it into his bowl for him. The combined smell of paprika and beef rose. Pristine, white cubes of potato soaked in the glistening, red broth. He was ravenously hungry.

"Good appetite," the fat man told him, and added something indecipherable to the waiter.

"Egészségedre," the men around him said, lifting their glasses.

"Egészségedre," Harkályi repeated. He held the Unicum under his nose, then watched the other men swallow their own portions whole. They smiled and urged him onward, and he obliged them. The liquid tasted like burned rubber, and then like rotten vegetation. The other men laughed. "That is awful," he told them.

"Maybe," the fat man said, "but it is Hungarian."

The three of them stood from the table. They left a small pile of colorful bills, and exited with a few awkward salutations. The steam rose from his goulash, which he ate feverishly. From a straw basket he removed a slice of fresh bread, of házikenyér, the likes of which he had often believed he would never again taste. When the waiter passed, Harkályi caught his eye and asked for another serving of Unicum.

5.

The stew in his belly, he feared, would not keep him warm for any good duration, so he walked quickly. His true destination, the great Dohány synagogue, which stood in the opposite direction, would wait for him as it had done so patiently and without complaint for so many years; it was expecting him. He will deliver the stone he carried in his pocket, an offering that will signify, to him, the distance that existed between remembering and never forgetting. First, however, he must see the Danube or, more correctly, the Duna.

He wound his way along crowded streets made cavernous by tall residential buildings that emitted a singular blue light from a thousand windows. A whole nation lay asleep in a bath of commercial entertainment.

In the absence of streetlamps, the glow filled the path before him for several paces, then plunged him again into a different kind of darkness. The hue of the entire street changed by degrees with every new televised scene, growing brighter and then darker again, and even darker and brighter yet. He carried himself, so he believed, directly toward the river.

The streets did not align themselves to a grid but rather to some circular logic of their own, and they certainly were not designed to accommodate this number of parked cars. The narrowness and curvature of the roads necessitated the haphazard distribution of automobiles, all of them small—Lada, Yugo, Fiat, Trabant—upon the sidewalks, and he was forced to either walk in the road, a dangerous proposition, surely, although the traffic appeared to have ceased for the night, or to maneuver his aging frame through an obstacle course of bumpers and side-view mirrors. The lawlessness was intolerable, yet he attempted to maintain a lively, brisk pace in an effort, amply rewarded thus far, to retain the warmth of the coffee house. It was a wonder that the entire city didn't sink under its own vehicular weight. As a child he had spent considerable time underground, hiding from the Arrow Cross. He pictured the entire surface of the city giving way, crumbling and cascading down into the cellars and catacombs of Pest, where he once subsisted on the furtive scraps that friends of Kodály could, on occasion, deliver to him, often at the risk of their own well-being.

Harkályi did not encounter another pedestrian until he reached the embankment, although several taxi cabs passed him, slowly, attempting to entice him out of the winter air. The taste of paprika remained on his tongue, warmed him, until he emerged at the left bank of the Duna. He was farther upstream than he had anticipated, just below the Chain Bridge. Directly opposite him was Castle Hill, its dome aglow in buttery lights. To the left of it stood Gellért Hill, adorned by a statue of a woman who once held up a cog seemingly taken from some monstrous machine.

When communism fell, she exchanged it for a leaf of some variety, clearly plucked from an equally monstrous tree.

He had spent many similar nights, at this very hour, walking along this river in Vienna, yet here it both was and was not the same river. To him it will always be the Duna, not the Donau or even the Danube. The Duna. All Hungarian history was steeped in it, as was that of his own family. The wind was harsh, but also comfortingly recognizable and sonorous. The river smelled of rust and, he had to admit, familiarly, faintly, of urine. There was also blood in the air. Somewhere around here, likely over on the Buda side, in front of the Gellért Hotel, his grandparents, unfit to travel, were gunned down, their bodies left to the vagaries of the tide while, in the hotel, men and women, naked and segregated, took the waters of the mineral-rich thermal springs seeping from the fault lines at the foot of the Buda Hills. His family tried to assimilate—they changed their name from Specht to Harkály, and, soon thereafter, at the advice of some kindhearted neighbors, to the more grammatically plausible Harkályi. His father left for a forced-labor camp convinced that those same neighbors were responsible for turning him over to the authorities.

For all of these many years, Harkályi longed to stand again at this river, to feel in his chest its peculiar, bitter stench. He breathed heartily, and was comforted. He owned nothing belonging to his grandparents except for this stone, which he considered throwing in after them, returning it to them here at their grave. From his parents, he possessed only a simple melody, which they often hummed and half-sang to him and his brother, and to each other. The next day, in the final measures of his new opera, he would share that song with the entire world.

6.

The only people fit to wander the embankment at that hour were lonely, world-weary old men and the prostitutes who preyed upon them.

Harkályi walked slowly north, against the tide, along the wide promenade and past a pack of hyenic street hustlers who eyed him hungrily but maintained a distance. The fading red embers of an unfiltered cigarette landed in his path, and there was giggling. He extinguished it in stride and with satisfaction. Experience told him that there existed many ways to prostitute oneself, and he had reason to suspect that the bartering of one's physical self was the least spiritually demanding of them. He pitied these shivering, desperate boys, but also envied them.

He passed a series of luxury hotels, their riverfront patios closed for the night, if not for the season. Budapest had grown wealthy. The stone lions at the base of the Chain Bridge greeted him like old friends. As a boy, he named them Scylla and Charybdis; between them, on the other side, a traffic tunnel led beneath the castle and toward the promised freedom of Western Europe. Sadly, these were not the same lions from his childhood, but reproductions, their offspring. As the Red Army wrested control of Budapest, the Nazis destroyed all of the bridges over the Duna, waiting until rush hour to do so. By that time, Harkályi was already convalescing in a Vienna hospital, awaiting, per Kodály's arrangement, a personal visit from Anton von Webern himself. There was talk of a temporary post at Radio Vienna. When neither the visit nor the position materialized, the latter of which he did not particularly covet, he left for America without telling his mentor and continued his studies at a conservatory in Philadelphia. For years thereafter, his letters to Kodály were returned to him unread, except, he suspected, by the Soviet censors.

Farther along, a two-lane road ran between the parliament building and the river, but there was no sidewalk, so Harkályi stayed close to the small, stone ledge along which a guardrail prevented him from falling into the river. Three feet below him, driftwood and dead birds populated the crevasses of jagged boulders. Sentries in formal uniforms stood outside a pair of outhouse-like structures at either end of the white parliament building. They held machine guns, and eyed him even more ferociously than had the hustlers. The massive structure itself was difficult to see from this angle, but Harkályi remembered that it was every bit as spectacular as Notre Dame or the British parliament building, which was to say that it appeared simultaneously majestic and artificial, more a sculpture than a building that might be occupied. He could not comprehend the immensity of the detail; it was too much to look at, and he discovered that it could best be seen only peripherally, from the corner of his eye, in small chunks that, were they placed together, would dizzy him even further. "Frozen music," as Goethe called architecture, was not quite the correct term. Music *represented*—it could be about something; architecture just *was,* and this building was even more so. The distinction embarrassed Harkályi in some way. He did not want to look at it; it was too beautiful, a monument to itself alone.

A flat transport ship appeared from beneath the Margit Bridge ahead of him, and he stopped to watch it pass. The sound of the engines was incredible, like an entire factory dedicated to the production of ball-peen hammers and garbage-can lids. It was lovely, really. Only a single, faint lightbulb illuminated the cabin, making the vessel all but invisible. The noise conquered everything around it, the city and its entire history; when it receded, he heard one of the parliament guards yelling at him. The young man approached, his machine gun drawn, and Harkályi pictured his own swollen body floating downstream, in the wake of this ship, to the grave of his grandparents. He did not understand what the soldier said, but interpreted the message, delivered by the angry motion of the gun's barrel, and continued his walk upstream, more briskly this time. Half-expecting the sound of gunfire, he did not turn around.

Past the parliament building, an electric tram line followed the bank of the river. From the platform, a sidewalk continued to the Margit Bridge. On it, above his head, two underdressed ladies noisily made their way back toward Pest. They were on the körút, the very same road on which his hotel was located, only a few blocks away. He crossed through a small park situated under the base of the bridge, up a ramp to the road. The women had disappeared, mere ghosts. Sleep will not come tonight, he knew, not restful sleep at any rate, so instead he awaited the next passing taxi, which would take him to Dohány Street, to the synagogue.

7.

The synagogue was on fire. The realization descended upon him slowly, like an illness. The streets were emptied, the windows of the nearby apartments darkened. He assumed at first that the smoke rising from the triangular roof, between the Moorish domes, emanated from a chimney. He pictured a servant inside polishing the silver, mopping the floors, perhaps a zealous rabbinical student pouring through the library for the single arcane utterance, marginalized to some forgotten, dust-strewn alcove, that will help him make sense of his life, still so very young. Even when the first yellow flames danced into view, they appeared as an apparition, a flashback to the final days of his childhood in Budapest. Only the sound roused him: a violent crack like the report of a Luger aimed just centimeters above his head.

His shock—and it was shock now, not precisely fear just yet—found expression in a throaty scream, one unburdened by the demands of meaning. It was the sound, not entirely foreign to Harkályi, of pure terror. The noise carried through the expanse of buildings, down Dohány Street.

He did not know the Hungarian word for fire, so he yelled, "Fire!"

No reaction came from the blank wall of concrete and glass opposite the synagogue. It was the largest in Europe and occupied a parcel of land on which Herzl himself once lived. Flames climbed higher, fueled by the fierce March wind, and they chewed up a tile roof that one would not have expected to burn so readily.

Harkályi shuffled to the doorways across the street, pressed all of the intercom buttons at once, producing a melody of electronic burps and bleeps. "Fire!" he yelled. Surely those on the third and fourth floors could see that the roof was on fire, that fire was consuming the synagogue. The sound of it grew louder, steadily more vicious. He ran to the next doorway and pressed all of the buttons on the metallic interface until he found the word: "Tűz!"

"Tűz! Tűz!"

He entered a glass Matáv booth, but the phone would not function without a pre-paid calling card and he was ignorant of the local version of 911. He smashed the receiver with all of his strength against the glass shell of the booth, but it refused to break. A pain carried through his arm and landed in his shoulder. Outside again, he removed the stone from his pocket and hurled it at the phone booth. The sound was amazing, like a crystal chandelier plunging, mid-performance, into an open concert-grand piano. He carefully rescued the stone from the rubble, wiped it off with his gloves, and returned to pressing random codes into the communication and locking mechanisms of the nearby apartment buildings. "Fire! Help!"

Lights finally blinked on in the windows above. Angry oaths landed on him as if from overturned chamber pots, until the fire became blindingly obvious. A chorus picked up the refrain of "Tűz! Tűz!" until the entire block was alight. Men streamed from the buildings in their blue-and-white MTK Budapest sweatpants. A groggy crowd formed. The sidewalk itself opened to reveal a storage cellar. The smell of the basement, identical to those in which he had once hid, caused Harkályi's racing heart to stop for an instant. A ladder flew out, then was raced across the street and pressed against the façade of the synagogue, where the flames had spread to the columns supporting the domes.

With practiced efficiency, two dozen men got to synchronous work. One of them climbed the ladder, next to which five more men erected a scaffold with a pulley system to lift pails of water. A line formed across the street, into the foyer of one of the apartment buildings. Harkályi joined their ranks, dead in the center of Dohány Street. Heavy buckets of water came one after the other out of the building and were passed along the line. He took them in his right hand and twisted to deliver them to the next man, who rewarded him with an empty one traveling the opposite direction, slightly less fast, away from the burning building. Harkályi could not keep up. He could no longer breathe, and he slowed the entire chain, further endangering the synagogue he had traveled so far to visit. The air would not leave his chest; it expanded into a painful knot beneath his ribcage and he grew faint, staggered on his feet. The young man next to him said something he couldn't understand. A woman appeared, took him by the arm, and led him to the curb, where he sat. The rescue operation continued seamlessly in his absence. The cold winter air found the perspiration that glued his clothes to his body and he started to shiver. The woman returned after a moment and handed him a tiny cup made of green ceramic. "Tessék," she said, and he smelled the pálinka before she even poured it from a plastic bottle, its Coca-Cola label still intact.

"Thank you," Harkályi answered, breathless. "Köszönöm szépen."

"Nem Magyar?"

"Amerikai vagyok."

"Igen, amerikai?"

"Igen."

Another woman appeared with a blanket, which she wrapped over his shoulders. The liquor, a kind of homemade slivovitz, tasted surprisingly delicious; it prickled the lining of his chest, his stomach. He regained control of his breathing, and either from the booze or the embarrassment at his age and physical ineptitude, he felt his face glowing bright red. The women had further work to do and left him alone to watch the spectacle. The full buckets appeared from the foyer of a house and passed through the hands of twenty men, many of them half Harkályi's age, and then were attached by their handles to a large hook and hoisted up using the pulley; the empty ones were tossed down to a man on the ground and fed back into the line. It was beautiful. Harkályi expected the men to break out in song. Every so often, the man closest to the roof would climb down and allow another to take over, to plunge his face into the smoke and to throw water at the flames, which neither subsided nor spread. A small carload of reporters and photographers arrived to document the men working in unison like an efficient, steaming machine. Harkályi made a mental note of the rhythm.

Sirens nipped at the edges of his hearing, still excellent despite the years, and soon some small degree of relief washed over the crowd. Exhaustion by then slowed even the younger men, yet they continued to pass the metal buckets back and forth. The sound of the fire brigade, which grew steadily louder, reminded him of the wartime air raid sirens, sounds once heard so frequently that they eventually lost all currency. The real danger came not from falling bombs or the buildings that collapsed under the weight of fire, but rather from the bitter Gentiles those bombs sent scurrying to join him underground. The mobs of desperate, anti-Semitic citizens were all-too-ready to denounce lifelong friends of the family, for only a tin of sardines as the reward. One ill-timed sneeze and young Lajos would have found himself unearthed and exiled—or worse.

There were fates more capricious and incomprehensible than exile.

The stone in his pocket, now collecting the sweat of his labors, was the only remaining totem of his childhood. Even Tibor had passed on; his brother, by some series of miracles, survived the war and the camps, but succumbed to a drunken gambler, newly destitute, swerving his way back to the city on the Atlantic City Expressway, and left Magda to Harkályi's absentee care. The stone survived when everything else around him withered, and it traveled with him from Hungary to

Czechoslovakia, Czechoslovakia to the U.S. Army hospital in Vienna, and then to London and, eventually, Philadelphia.

He will leave the stone here at the Tabac-Schul, where it can, like him, complete its journey. It had never, in all of these many years, felt so unbearably heavy.

8.

The sirens grew louder until three red trucks arrived, followed closely by a black sport utility vehicle full of rabbis and their bodyguards. Blue and red lights spun and danced around Harkályi, reflecting in the windows of the synagogue and the buildings facing it. What a scene! As the firemen emerged, the neighborhood men scurried to the safety of the sidewalk, where Harkályi climbed to his feet. Bottles of fresh wine appeared, and he drank heartily from every one that was passed. Photographers clamored for the attention of the sweating men. They did not recognize Harkályi, for which he was grateful. The crude, homemade alcohol burned his stomach, but helped to calm his nerves. The fire, although seemingly contained, continued to destroy the synagogue roof. The firemen uncoiled their hoses and dragged them toward the burning building. Reporters with television cameras positioned the rabbis with their backs to the synagogue and interviewed them with smoke rising behind them. One of them wept openly and the cameraman handed him a handkerchief.

The apartment doors remained open so that the men could go upstairs to see the effects of their labors from the upper floors. Harkályi followed them through the cramped foyer and up a series of stone steps. The climb was not difficult, now that he had regained his breath and found strength in the fresh Bikavér wine—the so-called bull's blood—still being passed freely around. A woman stood in the threshold, the one who had brought him the blanket, which he handed back in return. "Csókolom," he said to his hostess—I kiss your hand—and she giggled at the formality. The men did not remove their shoes, and they splashed mud across the wooden floors.

"You are an American, yes?" someone asked. It was the man who was next to him in line, the woman's husband.

"Yes," Harkályi said. "Do you speak English?"

"No, a little. But my wife."

"Your Hungarian is very good," she said. She was perhaps thirty years old, wearing a morning jacket over her long nightdress. She placed the blanket over her own shoulders.

"Look at the roof," she said, taking him by the hand. The apartment was small, but beautifully furnished with antiques apparently inherited from several generations of ancestry, if such a thing were possible. A child slept on a divan, impervious to the commotion and conversation in the room, a corner of which served as their dining area. Books covered an entire wall and neighbors congregated in the tall windows, which opened to a balcony overlooking the synagogue. The firemen sprayed a material the color and consistency of fake snow.

To his surprise, the damage to the roof was minimal, perhaps only cosmetic.

"I don't understand," Harkályi said. The neighbors, less impressed, trickled slowly back to their own homes. "I saw the flames. It's a miracle."

The firemen now used water, at very high pressure, to wash away the foam. It looked as if it were raining, but only on one small parcel of one street.

"They do this every holiday and every election," her husband said.

"You mean it was arson?" Harkályi asked. They looked at him blankly. "Someone did this on purpose, set the synagogue on fire?"

They smiled, almost amused, as if at a precocious child. "Of course," the man said. "The skinheads."

"This is how they celebrate Independence Day in Hungary," his wife said.

The pálinka and wine began to make Harkályi dizzy. His knees shook. He wanted very much to sit down, but the man's wife yawned and pulled the blanket more closely around herself.

"It's late—I must go," Harkályi said. "Thank you for the wine."

"You're welcome," the young man told him, leading him to the door. "Enjoy your holiday."

The stairwell was frigid and he was ready, almost, to return to his hotel. Outside, the firemen were putting away their gear and the crowds had gone to bed. He stared in awe at the pristine roof, which he so recently saw destroyed before his very eyes. It was practically unscathed. He had witnessed a miracle. For a moment, only a flashing moment that he would promptly regret, he considered throwing his stone at one of the elaborate windows of the synagogue, simply because he expected it would bounce off. The stunning beauty of the building was made even more profound, to him, by its permanence, as ineradicable as the Earth itself.

Freezing halfway to his death, he allowed the stone to remain in his pocket while he walked slowly back to the körút, sustained only by the alcohol in his blood, to hail a cab. A gregarious and hirsute driver engaged him in a lengthy conversation he didn't understand, or even hear above the Gypsy music rattling in the speakers behind his seat. "Igen," Harkályi told him. "Tudom, tudom." I know, I know.

9.

Even with the smoke and the grime scrubbed from his face and drained down into the belly of the city, sleep remained an impossibility. He lay down nevertheless to welcome the voices he knew to expect. He did not fear them now, in the gentle twilight of his unconsciousness. In a matter of hours, he would loosen on the world his new opera, *The Golden Lotus*.

Again, he will take the songs of his family, of his people, of his fellow prisoners at Terezín, and share them with the fickle-minded public, who will purchase copies but, he knew, never really *hear* them.

He could already picture before him hundreds of thousands of shiny DVDs, and hear the corresponding number of dead souls calling, admonishing him, encouraging him. So much music had been lost, more notes than he could draw in this lifetime or in a hundred of them. The faces wanted Harkályi to speak for them, and it was a responsibility that weighed heavily, much too heavily, upon him. He must answer to them first, and only then to himself.

Harkályi had kept private, until then, only one final element of his being, but come the last measures of his new opera, even his parents' lullaby will become another morsel for public consumption.

These half million compact discs were perfect reproductions of each other, but in the hands of his public they will reflect a half million different realities. Each will be unique, every spin through the home high-fidelity system a new event, a new experience for the listener. Recorded music changed over time, but nothing could exhume the spectral presence of a living performance. The concert hall had become a sacred place, as sacred in some ways as where he learned to compose music.

It had become impossible now to comprehend such a thing, but the hideous truth remained that it was Zoltán Kodály himself who suggested that Lajos, a thirteen-year-old violin prodigy, should wait out the remainder of the war in the Terezín ghetto. Better there, he had thought, than fending for scraps in the sub-basements of Budapest.

Almost 250 years earlier, Joseph II had ordered the construction of an outpost at the confluence of the Ohře and Labe rivers, the first line of defense protecting the Austrio-Hungarian Empire from the savage Germanic hordes. Across the Ohře from the small fortress, in which, more recently, the regicide Gavrilo Princip perished, stood the spa town of

Terezín. The Nazis offered that village, Kodály had told him, to the Jewish population of Central Europe as a safe haven, sequestered from the general population. A former Liszt Academy colleague, immediately upon his arrival, had sent Kodály a postcard boasting of the vast and vibrant musical life that flourished under the protection of the administrative council of Jewish elders. Karel Ančerl himself conducted a resident orchestra. Wealthy Jews from all over Central Europe, denied their civil rights and freedom of movement at home, funneled toward Czechoslovakia.

Budapest was no longer safe. Lajos's father had not been heard from since his departure for forced labor at a brick factory someplace beyond the city limits. With the blessings of their mother, Kodály made arrangements, at tremendous personal expense, to have Lajos and his brother, Tibor, smuggled safely to Vienna. One June evening, at dusk, they emerged from the cellar beneath Andrássy Boulevard, where they had been hiding from the Arrow Cross. His mother, always graceful, did not cry as they were hoisted into the bed of a horse-drawn wagon. She handed Lajos a sack of walnuts and a smooth, round stone he could use to break them open. He would not see her again, though her voice still rang in his ears. It would be her song that the world would hear decades later, in the afternoon. "Do not be afraid," she had said. As they pulled away, she sang to them, and to herself, a gentle lullaby.

The boys hid for hours beneath a bed of straw and manure, stopping finally, before dawn, in Vienna. They had already eaten all of the nuts, three days' worth, yet Lajos held fast to the stone and would continue to do so for more than half a century. In Vienna, or near it, they waited in lines that extended to the very horizon, until a small pack of bored German officers chose which among them to herd aboard two vacant boxcars. A soldier pulled the paperwork from his hands, and Lajos and his brother were permitted to join 150 others on Transport No. IV/141 from Vienna; a far greater number, most of them elderly and infirm, remained behind. The endless clip-clop syncopation of the locomotive disgorged from the passengers a hideous music of moaning and sobbing, of death itself, that could not be notated by human hands. It was hours or days—perhaps a month, or ten years, or a thousand—before they reached Terezín, a town that he and Tibor and so many others would come to regard as the anteroom to hell itself.

Harkályi rose from his soft bed, entirely unrested, and closed the bathroom door behind him. The joints of his elbows and knees ached; there was pain in his lower back. The steam of the shower warmed his naked body, the skin that hung loosely from his arms and belly, while he scrubbed the debris from one eye and then the other. His wooly, normally wild hair was shorn close and tame for the events of the day about to unfold before him.

10.

The faint daylight oozing through the ceiling of clouds made the temperature even more jarring. It felt colder that morning than it had in the middle of the night, when he had been drenched in sweat. Harkályi avoided looking at the picture of himself staring out at him again from the window of the record shop, which was not yet open for business. Perhaps it was closed in honor of Independence Day; it was difficult to say—everything was different now in Hungary. It felt like snow might fall soon.

The sidewalks of the körút were full of people, many of them already intoxicated. He had by mistake left his wristwatch in the room. Over at the National Museum, they were already reenacting Petőfi's speech of March 15, 1848, when the poet spoke out against the empire and instigated a revolt that failed to gain from Austria the independence that Hungary so desperately desired and would not earn until the end of the Soviet regime. If even then. There were speeches, nationalistic hymns, a brass band. Children waved flags while men passed bottles of pálinka through the smoking crowd. Harkályi had seen the ceremonies on satellite television and had no desire to witness them in the flesh.

In the underpass beneath the Nyugati train station, a band of South Americans in colorful attire performed cheerful, primitive music in a circle, to the delight of passersby. Waves of people spilled from the metro's escalators. The woman from whom he bought the hóvirág was not present, but in her place others sold onions and roasted pumpkin seeds. A pretty young girl sold wrinkled clothes from a laundry hamper. A freshly shaven youth attempted to hand Harkályi a religious pamphlet, but he recoiled from the boy's reach.

He had time to waste before meeting Magda and wanted to take a stroll, to clear his head before the concert, an event lingering ominously at the furthermost poles of his thoughts; he knew it was there, yet refused, still, to bring it into focus. It was embarrassing—the pageantry and applause, the idolatry that conflated him, this tired old man, with his compositions. He could not wait to see his niece; she alone would relieve the tedium of public appearance.

The flower shop was not open. He would have liked to buy a new bouquet for Magda. He scanned the headlines at the newsstand, but there was no front-page mention of the synagogue fire. Perhaps it was old news, as those neighbors said, that arson occurred every year at this time. It was unfathomable that fascism, even a sickening, modern parody of it, could continue to exist in the twenty-first century. No frame of reference existed any longer, except in the minds and art of his quickly deteriorating generation. People did not understand what had transpired.

Above the clapping and pan-fluting of the South Americans, he was able to discern some kind of commotion emanating from a hallway leading to the rear of the train station: the prolonged, rapid-fire clinking of a slot machine. There was cheering, a crowd forming. A shabby man, older in appearance than his age would dictate, with the gray pallor of lifelong drunkenness, had won a small fortune in coins. His excitement infected all of those within the glass-enclosed pub, as well as those outside, their noses pressed against the filthy windows. The man bought three liters of wine, which the scantily clad server ladled from vats built into the surface of the bar. She handed unstemmed drinking glasses to all present, and more people crammed their way inside to partake of the free alcohol. It was a minor stampede of the borderline homeless. It looked like the greatest day in the entire life of the winning man; he would tell stories of this morning for the short remainder of his dull life. The scene sickened Harkályi, but fascinated him also. He envied the men's easy camaraderie, so utterly free of pretense.

Farther down the hall, he happened upon a sight so foreign that he questioned if he had fallen asleep after all, if it were but a dream shaken loose from the recesses of his memory. No, it was real. A band of skinheads—true skinheads, in the flesh, six or seven of them—were attacking a Negro man without stop, without mercy. Blood drooled from the young man's eyelids, from his lips. They kicked at him from all sides.

"Stop that!" Harkályi ordered them, before he could think better of it.

The smallest of the assailants, no more than sixteen years old, approached with the silver blade of a serrated knife drawn. He said something in Hungarian, his voice cracking. His armband did not feature a swastika but, instead, a green machinery cog. They stood toe-to-toe, but this boy was half a foot shorter. Harkályi craned his neck to look into the dusty-glass color of the child's eyes. He could not find it in himself to be afraid. The noise of the gamblers behind him swelled, drew closer. The skinheads dropped their prey and shouted at the child, whose vodka breath polluted his own; the boy lifted Harkályi's necktie and ran his knife through it, dragging it downward to split the silk into shreds. "Zsidó disznó," he said—words Harkályi would look up two days later, when he arrived again in Philadelphia; he knew better than to ask Magda.

"Jewish pig." The boy backed away, and stepped on the fallen man as the skinheads retreated into the depths of the train station.

The drunken revelry spilled out of the pub and into the hallway. The bums laughed and cheered and ignored the unconscious black man. Harkályi knelt next to him, dirtying his own pants. The man's jacket read U.S. ARMY and GIBSON over the left breast. There was not as much blood as he had thought, though his face had already started to mutate into some hideous mask: one eye had sealed entirely closed under the weight of a large lump on his brow, his nose appeared broken, and a safety pin affixed to a tiny Hungarian flag jutted out of his bottom lip. When Harkályi removed it, the man regained consciousness.

"The fuck happened?"

"You were attacked by skinheads," Harkályi told him. "Wait here and I will get a doctor."

"I don't need a doctor. Help me up."

Harkályi attempted to lift the man, but he was surprisingly heavy for his diminutive stature. He was solid muscle, but his neck could not fully support the weight of his own head. It was only with significant struggle that he was able to at last climb to his feet.

"You are an American?" Harkályi asked.

The man did not respond, except by way of a deep-bellied groan. Saliva and blood dripped freely from his mouth.

"You need medical help. Please."

"I said I don't want a doctor, old man. Did you say skinheads?"

"Yes. Today, apparently, is their big occasion to go wild, or even wilder than usual."

"I guess so," the man said. The pain must have been excruciating. It was a wonder that he had the strength to stand. "I need to go. Thanks for your help."

"Of course. Are you certain you do not want me to find a doctor?"

"No, I'm good."

The man carried himself toward the crowded underpass. Harkályi watched his slow, ambling progress. He still smelled the alcoholic stench of that murderous child; his was the very face of Harkályi's own parents' murderers, whom he had loathed since he hid in those underground passages so similar to this one. Only now Harkályi was not angry—his lifetime's worth of fury had dried up, and he mustered only some sensation approaching pity for the boy. It was ignorance, as much as evil, that made him dangerous. And it was the joy in his own heart, and the forgiveness, that distinguished them. He removed his ruined tie and left it on the ground, in the small pool of spilled blood.

II.

With an hour yet before he had to depart for Buda, he sat on the plush hotel sofa to watch television. There was no news, only reenactments of previous events, the cyclical return of war and famine and genocide, war and famine and genocide, interrupted by equally crude commercial advertisements. Only the longitudes changed, and now it was the Americans who put men in concentration camps. Harkályi, to his regret, will not live long enough to hear the music composed in Guantánamo, or in these secretive black sites speckled like cancerous moles on Europe's backside.

Miraculously, the stories concerning the tremendous musical life of Terezín proved to be true, yet every other storied detail about that concentration camp—and it was most certainly a concentration camp—proved to be willfully exaggerated, if not criminally false. The Schutzstaffel used the site as a model facility, as the set of an elaborated staged drama demonstrating to the world their kindly treatment of Europe's Jews who, in reality, were upon arrival stripped of their possessions, shaved and deloused, and forced to live no better than oxen in prison-like dormitories.

When Lajos and his brother arrived in June of 1943, preparations had already begun for an inspection of the facilities by the Red Cross. To prevent the appearance of overcrowding, additional labor engagement transports were loaded and quickly dispatched at all hours of the night and day, carrying up to a thousand people at a time to Poland and places unknown. Rumors filtered back, slightly less quickly, even among the children, and presumably to the entire world, about the nature of those steady departures. He and Tibor could have been condemned at any time. The kapo of their dormitory provided them with a postcard on which they were to inform their family about the comfortable conditions in which they found themselves. They did not use Kodály's address, for fear of raising suspicion among the authorities about his activities on their behalf, and instead they had the card sent to their former neighbors, the ones who had alerted the Nazis to their whereabouts and had had their father arrested; the boys hoped that the Arrow Cross would deliver it personally and arrest them as Jewish sympathizers. Only years later, during his previous visit to Hungary, would Harkályi learn that Kodály and his wife had by that time already abandoned their home for the dank basement of a Budapest church, where he completed his *Missa Brevis*.

The Red Cross arrived, and then departed again, and tens of thousands more souls continued to Poland.

There existed in Terezín any number of ensembles, tolerated by the Nazis and consisting of rotating rosters of musicians, who performed everything from complete operas—almost exclusively German and Italian—to decadent, American-style jazz. A small town square contained a wooden riser, upon which they performed public concerts on weekends. There was even a baby grand piano, albeit a crippled one, its legs shorn off as if it had stepped on a landmine. Most of the serious musical activities occurred in secret, however. As a "millionaire," camp slang for a new prisoner, and at his age, Lajos was not at first provided access to one of the many violins circulating through the town, some of them carried to Czechoslovakia unassembled and glued roughly back together. He and Tibor were assigned to the Halfsdienst, a work detail for young people, but were also permitted to participate in a children's chorus. The boys learned to speak some Czech despite the proclamation that all public utterances were to be in German. In his precious free time, late in the night, Lajos transcribed for violin, from memory, Bartók's *Fourteen Bagatelles* and performed them on a borrowed instrument, eventually allowed him, for a small but enthusiastic audience in the attic of the dormitory in which he lived.

When word of his musical prowess spread, as it was bound to do in such a setting, he was given the regular use of a too-small, half-sized violin, on which he was able to practice for the occasional private violin lesson. He also found himself relieved of his work duties and, to the ire of his jealous brother, assigned to the exclusive group of Notenschreiber who reproduced by hand the rare, precious scores that arrived at Terezín, or were composed there amidst the chaos and horror. Every so often, Lajos would change a note or two, such as those at the very center of the violin part of Gideon Klein's *Trio,* and await with great joy his surreptitious contribution to the public performances. Many of those scores were lost, and little by little Harkályi had, in the intervening years, attempted to resurrect them in his own compositions.

12.

His mother sat alone, a porcelain cup of weak tea held on a saucer in her lap. The room was strangely bright, bleached by a sun that had drawn inexplicably closer. He approached her, as if dreaming, finally asleep, and as she stood, her smile grew bountiful enough to rid Lajos of all that plagued him. The porcelain made no sound as she returned it to the table.

"You made it," she said.

"Yes. Yes—I have made it."

"Let me look at you."

She took his shoulders in her hands and could tell how thin he had grown, that the meat had atrophied and shriveled from his bones. But her arms around him—this was why he had come. The tears swelled in his eyes. "I am so happy. So happy to see you." He held onto her so that she could absorb all of his suffering and sleeplessness, as if her youthfulness and beauty would make it dissipate like smoke.

"You are so thin," Magda said, "but you look healthy."

Neatly attired strangers murmured around her in countless languages about the current state of Europe, about these awful, dreadful times, about what new travesties today would bring. They stirred cubes of refined sugar into their teacups and stabbed tiny forks at their plates. A young girl, not yet a teenager, wound her way through the labyrinth of tables, collecting soiled dishes.

"It's unbelievable. Have I told you that you look exactly like your grandmother?"

"Only every time I see you."

"She was—"

"—the most beautiful woman in Budapest."

"Are you mocking me, Magda?"

"Only a little, bácsi." She was his same height, if not slightly taller, and she kissed him on both cheeks. "How is your room?"

"Fine, fine. Very comfortable."

"Két cappuccino," she told a passing and disinterested waitress, and they sat. "The coffee here's great, ten times better than what we get down at the base. Are you hungry?"

"No, I had room service deliver some things. You should eat, however. Oh, and I'm terribly sorry. I bought you some hóvirág but, foolishly, I left them on the metro."

The resemblance was impossible to fathom. She was the same age, or very close to the same age, that his mother was when he and Tibor saw her for the last time. Even her voice carried a distinct and soothing similarity.

The cukrászda doubled in the morning as a dining room for guests of the hotel, and the characteristic odors of baking sugar and of stale coffee lingered in the atmosphere. The pastry chefs arrived with regularity behind the counter to load the glass display cases with decorative cakes and tortes and every manner of creamy, rich dessert. The array of treats fascinated and repelled him; that people would consume such junk was an outrage, but that such an ocean of options existed, and in Budapest, was cause for celebration.

The difference between communism and democracy, he came to believe in the course of his travels, could be witnessed in that very display case full of cakes. On his last visit, he had spent an afternoon at Café Gerbeaud, the famous coffee house on Vörösmarty Square. At that time, they had one variety of cake available, which was extremely dry and not very delicious, but which cost him only ten forints. That was communism. Now, he could choose from a hundred varieties of cake, but each cost one thousand forints. That was democracy. Europe had chosen to choose, but Harkályi feared that they accepted only the illusion of choice. The display case was a mirage, a distraction. They were deciding from among different combinations of the very same ingredients used to make that flavorless cake in 1967.

"What would you say to a serving of Somlói galuska?" he asked.

"Bácsi, it's not even noon yet."

"What better time." He, with some difficulty, got the attention of a waitress. "Somlói galuska."

She appeared to be surprised. "Igen?"

"Igen. Két."

"Kettő?"

“Igen, kettő.”

“Your Hungarian is returning.”

“Maybe one could say that I am returning to it. Perhaps that is why I am so nervous.”

“Nervous? You’ve been through this a million times.”

“Yes, and a million times I have been nervous. I cannot tolerate the pageantry involved with these events, yet I cannot avoid them because—”

“Because you are the ‘world’s greatest living composer.’”

“I have told you to stop that, Magdalene.”

“I’m only teasing. You’re not really the world’s greatest living composer.”

“Thank you.”

“This must be strange for you, being home. It’s been so long.”

“Since the death of Kodály, yes. It is strange. Do you know that last night I went to visit the synagogue and when I arrived it was on fire.”

“On fire? Was it destroyed?”

“No. No, and that’s the peculiar thing. With my own eyes I watched it burn and yet once the fire was extinguished, there was no damage at all. I know that I’m beginning to sound like a crazy old man, but I believe I witnessed a miracle, Magda.”

“A miracle, bácsi? There has to be some explanation.”

“Yes, of course you are right. Some explanation. I must admit that I have not thought of this city as ‘home,’ as you call it, but it *is* a joy to see you.” She leaned forward to kiss him on the side of his face. “I am afraid that I’m not very good company this morning.”

“Are you still having trouble sleeping?”

“Yes, sadly, but it’s always worst before a concert, much less before a premiere. But I am very deeply moved to see you. Before I get too sentimental, however, let’s try this galuska.”

She tapped at her eyes with a white napkin.

The cake—if that was the word for this bowl of unruly slop—looked awful; it was a mess of undercooked dough and runny chocolate sauce buried under whipped cream. The sight alone made his stomach turn.

"Perhaps this was not such a good idea after all."

"You have to at least taste it, bácsi."

"No—it's getting late. But tell me. You are working now for the American Army?"

"Our company is consulting for them. We're private contractors."

"War profiteers, you mean," he said, of course joking.

"Yes, in a way. We're integrating a suite of technical and logistical support systems into the military's preexisting network of security solutions."

"Network of security solutions?"

"Now who's teasing whom? I'm a translator. I assist the Hungarian security firms that the United States government hired to train the Iraqi police force."

"You're not serious. The Iraqi police?"

"We're teaching them the skills they'll need to relieve our soldiers of peacekeeping work in Iraq. My work will help them get home to their families faster."

"Why is this occurring in Hungary?"

"Cheap labor, basically. Our company works in six different security centers throughout the former Soviet Union. All these countries have mandatory military service, right? So these Hungarians are basically trained and disciplined already, not to mention eager for jobs."

"And you hire them to train Iraqi policemen?"

"On behalf of the United States government, right." She stirred a packet of artificial sugar into her coffee cup, and then leaned forward to whisper into his ear: "We're overseeing the interrogation of political prisoners from the Middle East."

Harkályi coughed. It was uncontrollable. In his haste for a drink, he nearly spilled his water glass. "Please excuse me," he said, taking a long drink. "I think it's time that I got dressed. There will be a car to meet us at one o'clock. I will feel fortunate to have a personal translator with me today. We will go to Buda for the concert, and then have some photographs taken with the prime minister. Now, however, please excuse me."

"I can't wait. In the meantime, have you seen a post office by any chance? I told my boyfriend I'd mail some letters for him."

"A boyfriend, Magda?"

"Yes, you'll meet him soon, I hope."

"I would like that very much. You should have brought him with you. Nothing is open today, of course. Perhaps you can find a mailbox."

"Of course. I'll do that, and be back before one. And then—a new opera! I'm so excited."

"It is not so new for me, Magda." He pushed the bowl of sugary goo away from his body and stood, with some effort. His knees no longer functioned as they once did. So much time had been stolen from him. "I will meet you downstairs. We will continue this conversation shortly. Seeing you, yes—it does almost feel as if I have come home. You are the last of the Harkályis, Magda."

"It's great to see you too. Just remember, you've been through this a million times before. Don't be afraid."

13.

Luck, a phenomenon that at age fourteen Lajos had already discerned as the afterthought of an indifferent God, one eclipsed from view in Bohemia, kept him and Tibor off those cattle cars bound for Poland and beyond the notice of the council of elders, whose unfortunate responsibility it became to condemn their fellow Jews to that passage across Mitteleuropa. While lethargy and apathy and incomprehension demagnetized the globe's moral compass, bodies continued to burn in the distance, the smoke rising to obscure the light of two million stars, still twinkling bright yellow, though already dead.

In the spring, a film crew arrived from Berlin to shoot a documentary that would be shown to the world. Karel Ančerl was ordered to prepare a special concert, with only a few days' notice, to take place on the main grandstand in the town center. It would include the *Study for Strings,* by Pavel Haas, and the children's opera *Brundibár,* by Hans Krása, both residents of Terezín and both major influences on Harkályi's earliest compositions.

Lajos copied the music with the promise that he would be granted the honor of performing with the second violins. The orchestra practiced around the clock, confident that their very lives depended upon a perfect performance. Haas and Krása attended every rehearsal to assist with certain questions of interpretation that arose, ecstatic that their music would gain a worldwide audience. Lajos's hands ached from the constant scribbling of notes, yet as he was frequently reminded, his suffering did not match that of his brother, whose tireless physical servitude to the kapo made him just as invaluable. Lajos's own hard work and dedication, rare for a musician of any age, endeared him to Ančerl.

In preparation for the film, and apart from the small circle of musicians otherwise occupied, every able-bodied woman and man—which is to say every woman and man, as those who were not of able body did not remain for long in Terezín—dedicated their labors to the beautification of the town. They added fresh coats of paint to the buildings and planted vast flower and vegetable gardens, though few among them would live to see them bloom again.

For days, the filmmakers shot images of children playing soccer, of families sitting around large, food-laden tables, of citizens in line to deposit fake money at the town's newly built bank. The world would see the glorious gift that the kaiser had given to the Jews—their own Edenic village, far from the devastation of the war. The concert would be equally farcical, with a row of plotted plants placed in an orderly line along the front of the stage to hide from the camera's view the shabby shoes that failed to match the dark, hastily tailored suits, each with a bright and prominent Star of David emblazoned on the chest.

On the morning of the performance, at the instruction of Ančerl, the concertmaster approached Lajos while he practiced his scales, a chore he relished for its distraction. The maestro had decided that he would not allow Lajos to perform in the concert. His cinematic debut would have to wait for another day, and for different circumstances. When asked why, he was told that he did not appear sufficiently Jewish to make the proper impression for the camera and, in addition, that his playing was simply not up to the standards of the adults in the string orchestra. If he wanted to become a concert violinist, he would have to dedicate himself to practicing more, without the distraction of copying music or notating the melodies that even then had started to ferment in his imagination. The disappointment stung; anger surged through his sunken frame, but he was powerless. The memory of that rage embarrassed Harkályi for the rest of his life. He had said some things out of youthful indiscretion that he will always regret.

He refused to attend the concert, and instead hid in the barracks. Tibor would later describe the event in detail, movement by movement, and in particular the immediate aftermath: once the camera stopped rolling, Ančerl with a wave raised all of the musicians to their feet and asked them to place their instruments on their chairs. He led the procession, baton still in hand, as they lined off the riser in single file, laughing at the joy of a successful performance. Men shook hands, grabbed proudly at their fashionable lapels. Smiling the entire way, they followed Ančerl's slow, funereal pace straight into the cars of the transport train, which already contained the families of every participant of the concert. Word quickly spread that they were being freed in recognition of their gift to the Reich, and they cheered and shouted to each other, despite the crowded conditions. At Auschwitz, so Harkályi learned many years later, only Ančerl among the hundreds of them would survive the day.

The maestro had rehearsed and conducted the concert, under the gaze of the cameras and of the entire world, with the full understanding that immediately afterwards he would lead the men in his charge to their deaths. In dismissing Lajos from the performance, Ančerl knowingly and deliberately saved his young life.

Twenty years later, Ančerl toured the United States and Harkályi, by then a professor of music in Philadelphia, though not yet internationally recognized, attempted to arrange a reunion. His letter to Ančerl was returned unopened by the management of the Czech Philharmonic, and he never spoke with the maestro again, not even after he emigrated to Canada.

"Goddamn Karel Ančerl," he had said back then, in Terezín. It was the first instance in his life that his prayers would be answered.

Lajos was left behind to rot, so he believed, while all of the other musicians and composers gained their freedom in Western Europe and elsewhere. He grew embittered, but also productive. With the sudden shortage of competent performers, the homesick guards approached him with commissions. They grew tired of hearing the same few marches, so they sent to Leipzig and Berlin and even Paris for new music—tangos and csárdás, arias from the latest operettas—which Lajos had to transcribe for a rotating cast of musicians and whatever instruments were on hand. The living could fill out the chords of the dead. He assigned all of the parts to all or to almost all of the musicians simultaneously, with only slight variations in form or timbre, so it didn't matter if he only had three violins or if his oboist had been shot, or even if there were no cello strings to be found within fifty miles. His inner ear grew accustomed to awkward variations in pitch, which he learned to incorporate into the music he composed based upon the Volkslieder the weeping officers sang drunkenly to him. The rapid turnover of musicians made it difficult to orchestrate precise melodies, so Harkályi taught himself a unique compositional style, a style that eventually gained him a vast, international following and brought him back here to Budapest after all of these years.

14.

They were sealed in a windowless, unadorned stone room in which two metal chairs had been placed before a table of colorful catered food. Sturdy padlocks prevented entry into the closets, where the priests hung their civilian clothes while saying mass. A sentry stood guard in the hallway, the personal bodyguard of the prime minister of the republic of Hungary, of Magyarország, who was said to be interned in an adjoining backstage cell. Magda picked at a strawberry, then at a misshapen cube of melon, while Harkályi paced in small, waltz-like circles.

"This melody you will hear at the very end, in the final string quartet—it is the lullaby that your grandparents sang to us."

"I remember. Papa would sing it too, but his voice was awful!"

"Perhaps not 'awful,' but what he lacked in talent he compensated for with volume."

"Yeah, that's definitely true." Magda's smile electrified him. "It's funny that your parents sang in Hungarian."

"They learned to sing before they learned how to speak. That was how they accumulated a vocabulary—one folk song at a time. It's such a tragedy. They believed they would be safe in Budapest."

"Papa didn't really talk about the war, but I heard him tell my mother once, when she was sick, that his parents—your parents—wouldn't have been safe anywhere. They were 'too vocal.' That was the term he used. That the best they hoped for was his safety and yours."

"Tibor was fearless, even as a boy, as strong as a bull."

"He always cried when he sang it."

"Yes, that is understandable, certainly. It was very painful for me to transcribe, and perhaps it was a mistake to do so."

"I can't wait to hear it."

"I cannot wait for this concert to . . . listen."

The orchestra had started to warm up, to arrive at a shared tuning. To Harkályi, the cacophony was gorgeous, like a summer meteor shower dripping from the heavens. There were sounds, often from the reeds and winds, that some listeners would consider unappealing, but in reality no awful voices truly existed—not even his brother's. The pre-musical chaos contained something honest, even truer than the manicured tones that would follow; it was music in the raw, free of false order, of linearity, and for that reason was ignored by the audience as if it were white noise. It was his favorite part of every concert. Colors and patterns of sound swirled forth from the altar, but were muted by the heavy wooden door.

His career as a composer was born, in a concentration camp, from hideous necessity. And it was in a concentration camp, now, that his beloved niece had gained employment. It was enough to make him weep. So like her grandmother, and so very and incalculably different. He wanted now to be alone, to fall to his knees and cry.

During the following weekend, the production of *The Golden Lotus* would be transferred across the river to the opera house, but Harkályi would not remain in Hungary long enough to witness the transition, or even to see for himself the Oriental-looking sets they constructed. He needed to return to his studio, to the empty staves that awaited him. Someday soon he would take on more composition students, when he felt confident that he had something to teach them. He would impart upon them the necessity of embracing the variety of willful ignorance that saw him through the greatest horrors that humanity can bestow, and which were responsible for this absurd celebrity. He will teach them to avoid the mistakes he had made. He will teach them to compose what they did not yet know and wished to understand.

There was silence, and then a faint knocking on the door. A young priest entered, without invitation, and gestured for them. "Tessék," he said. Harkályi stood before Magda, before the radiant image of his own mother. She brushed lint from the shoulders of his coat. The stone he carried felt weightless. It released him from its servitude. He lifted it into the fluorescent light of the small room. "Put this in your purse, Magda. It once belonged to your father. One day I hope you will understand what it is."

She took the stone from his hand, then smiled, though only faintly this time, confused, and kissed him on both cheeks. He was glad to be free of it.

"We should not keep them waiting any longer," Harkályi said.

The door was opened. In a single moment, no more than that, he would enter the swelling concert hall, the heart of this cold church, to accept the adulation of a thousand strange, howling faces, their teeth bared. Only then will he feel that he has arrived safely at what he might call home.

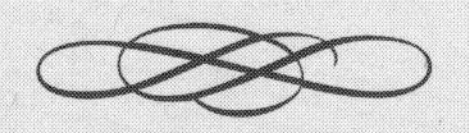

Brooking the Devil

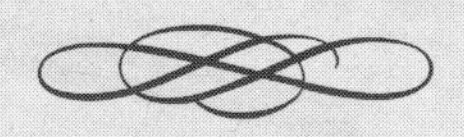

BROOKING THE DEVIL

I.

Brutus waited in the mess-hall line for twenty minutes, collected his grub, and sat facing the windows. He often went for days without speaking voluntarily to another soldier.

The men and women behind him, organized by race into table-sized ghettos, laughed and belched. He ate much too quickly and returned to his room. In the lull after breakfast the barracks remained more or less still while everyone shaved and shat or masturbated, if they could. The Army was putting something in the food. The huddled masses of soldiers and spies and torturers dissipated every morning at this time, quieting the hubbub almost to the point of nonexistence. Sparky was out, so Brutus had the room to himself. His bunkmate was a former seminarian from Massachusetts, and a punk. It came up on oh eight hundred and the sun still had not shown its ass. Five U.S. Marines were visiting from Budapest, and Brutus had to go fraternize, even though it was his only free day that whole week. But he had a few minutes, so he turned on the radio.

Brutus paid little attention to the Army Corps of Weather Prophets. They weren't calling for snowfall, but then again, they weren't calling for more war in the Balkans either. Or in the Middle East, for that matter. The government-sponsored stooges came on Armed Forces Radio with news of pending sunshine and brokered deals, sounding just like the spring training reports emanating from Florida. Hope sprang eternal. Back home, the Phillies signed another number-four starter; here, the Serbs signed another piece of anti-landmine legislation. Neither, Brutus knew, would last the season. The disembodied Voice of America also provided five minutes of English-language news at the top of every hour. It spoke of the lingering effects of a cyanide spill that had polluted the Tisza River and "devastated the livelihoods" of fishermen and chefs of Szeged's famous fish soup; there was an update on the ongoing debate, unresolved after a decade of legal mumbo jumbo in the Hague, about a dam on the Hungary-Slovakia border; and of course there was talk of more summits and of the bright prospects for eternal peace next door in the once and future Yugoslavia. America was at war with terror.

"Asshole," Brutus said, and switched the radio off.

In the eyes of the politicians and international tribunals, the prospects of long-term peace in the Balkans bore little relationship to the ongoing efforts of the civilian populations to establish their newly capitalistic lives—or to the army's perpetual presence here in the middle of nowhere. The ground rules changed after 9/11 and no one knew what to expect anymore. Oversight of the few U.S. Army bases remaining in Eastern Europe—far from the active theaters—fell through the administrative cracks. Things worked differently here, if they worked at all.

Brutus had been in Hungary for almost seven months and in all that time had not stepped foot out of Taszár. He didn't have clearance. The rec room had a high-def TV with a satellite hookup and a computer lab with e-mail and internet access, but letters from his sister Joan remained his main source of news from home. The rest of it was straight-up propaganda. She wrote once a week and sometimes sent books or magazines, which arrived with greasy thumbprints, or worse, pages sticking together. With a few minutes to spare, he reread her most recent letter. According to the postmark, it had only taken five days to reach him. People said that the frequent letters he sent home took about ten.

Joan's letter was handwritten in purple ink. "Dear Fancy Lad," it began.

"I think I told you that the Mambo has been talking about moving down South," his sister had written. "Do you remember that old bitch Blue Moon? Well she sold the house she was renting out over in

Roxborough and bought a shop of some kind down in Florida. She offered the Mambo a job and a place to live for free so I think she's going to go. She hates all this snow and cold weather here as much as I do. You're crazy the way you like this weather. Ha Ha Ha. I'll send you her new address when she gets down there but you should call her soon!

"Me and the boyz will be moving into her house and there's a room for you when you come home. James put all your books in boxes and they're already over there in the basement up on some wooden pallets for when it floods!"

The barracks came back to life and disrupted his concentration. Someone in the adjacent room shouted obscenities over his country music. Brutus stood up and locked the door. The footsteps and fag jokes and hillbilly guitar licks annoyed the living fuck out of him. All he wanted to do was read a goddamn letter. He looked at his watch. It was getting close to time.

"J. J. loves the backyard and he asks every day when you're coming over to play catch. I tried to get him to give up the army T-shirt like you asked me to but he wouldn't. His school has uniforms now though so he only wears it to bed and sometimes on weekends anyhow. James got a promotion and now he's learning how to make web pages. Did you get the e-mail he sent?"

Brutus checked his watch again and saw that he was going to be late.

Fuck it.

"I ran into Elvin and those guyz over at this new Mexican joint and they all said hello. He got a job now down at the casinos in A.C., not as a dealer but something like that he said. He was high but I think it was just some weed."

Brutus replaced the letter in the envelope and stood up. "Time to meet the marines," he said. In his jacket pocket he carried a paperback copy of *The Wretched of the Earth;* the Magyar Posta and many re-readings had tattered its corners and broken its spine.

Lieutenant Colonel Sullivan had invited a vanload of jarheads down from Budapest for what he billed as an informal information session. An unusual Big Brother program where troops from another service who had been in-country longer got to lead seminars on Adapting to Life in a Cinderblock Barn at the End of the Known World. Another group of marines, new arrivals from the Middle East, were temporarily stationed across the way in the base's restricted area, where by all unofficial accounts they were beating up Arabs in ways that made those Abu Ghraib photos look like souvenir shots from Sea World. Brutus wanted to get in there to see for himself.

Outside, there was no distinction between the clouds and the sky. They had a different kind of cold in Hungary than in America. A dry freeze penetrated everything and sucked all the moisture from his skin. The fatigues were useless, but Brutus didn't really mind the cold, not as much as most people. It was definitely going to snow.

Word on the street was that these marines from Budapest had the coziest gig in all of Europe, which was to say the coziest gig in the world. They patrolled the embassy in a city that wasn't exactly a hotbed of international terrorism—not yet anyway—and lived in some kind of mansion up on Castle Hill that overlooked the Danube and the parliament building. Apparently they had their own private bar complete with American whiskey and a pool table with red, white, and blue felt. Brutus had to hand it to the Hungarians: talk about keeping your friends close and your enemies closer. He found himself sympathizing more and more with the natives as his dissatisfaction with his own government grew. He took exception to the army's division of labor and, as an intellectual exercise, even flirted with Marxism now and then, but had yet to consummate the relationship. His presence in Hungary provided further evidence of capital's international expansion. That he had learned to appreciate the *Manifesto* while in the army made him understand why so many brothers had converted to Islam while in prison back in the sixties.

The marines were out of uniform but neatly dressed. They walked like roosters in a mating ritual, and each carried a big bottle of Jack Daniel's and grease-stained paper bags from McDonald's. There were five of them—a white guy, a Latino, and two brothers, along with a white staff sergeant, who said a few curt words of introduction. Brutus did his best to appear engaged. When the staff sergeant got done flapping his gums, everyone divided into groups and went inside. Though it wasn't expressly discussed, they split up along racial lines. The Latinos went to one room, the two sets of black people to two others. The staff sergeant and all the white men took the generals' executive lounge. Brutus followed an Uncle Sambo Marine named Doornail down the hall.

Everyone in the military got a nickname in basic training; it was one way to strip a man of his identity and replace it with one incapable of independent thought. No different than a slave being forced to adopt his master's name. Brutus already had his nickname when he signed up, and somehow it got picked up on the inside. His friends had called him Brutus as long as he could remember. The name was the only thing that he ever got from his father, but that didn't prevent Joan from calling him Fancy Lad, on account of what she considered his anal retentiveness, but what Brutus thought of as simple self-respect. He hated Doornail immediately for that very reason. No self-respect. He was another military nigger, America's modern equivalent of the house slave. Shuckin' and jivin'—and all too often dying—for the Man.

Brutus had joined the army in the first place because he had heard that it was easier for a black man to excel in the military than in any other profession. Without a college degree, he couldn't find decent work back in Philly, so he had enlisted. He did his research. The military was the first

American institution to get completely desegregated, and it was just about the only occupation where someone could advance on the basis of ability, regardless of race. But that was before he had read Fanon and *Captain Blackman*. Of course things didn't pan out the way the government had promised. Racism ran uncontested in the military just like everywhere else. Brutus had been passed over for promotion a bunch of times while white and even Latino soldiers of lesser talent moved past him. He came to realize that the army was just the Man's personal bodyguard, obligated to take a bullet so privileged college kids could continue to make money working at their daddies' offices and car dealerships. But he wasn't going to play the game, not like this Doornail punk in his Ralph Lauren shirt and pressed khakis. A rich-ass polo player riding a horse and swinging his stick at someone. Branded right on the black man's chest no less. Or the red, white, and blue of those Tommy Hilfiger clothes brothers wore in deference to the flag that kept them hungry. These men in their preppy clothes looked like white minstrel entertainers in blackface, but that was simpler for them than creating their own identities. The easy way out was the only way out for most of his friends back home. Join the army. March and dance for the Man.

And he fell for it.

Doornail placed the whiskey and cheeseburgers on the center conference table and the soldiers swarmed on them. The bottle got passed around despite the hour, and people talked about where they were from and what they thought of Europe so far. The marine baited them, trying to get them loosened up enough to talk shit about Sullivan. "I hear he's a punk," he said, but no one went for it. Brutus wanted to be back in his room. He didn't touch the food, but he helped himself to the whiskey when it came his way. He hated the implicit assumption that he could be made to feel at home by this marine's shit talk and fake jive. Semper fi? Semper idem, motherfucker. He could hear the staff sergeant and the white soldiers' laughter through the walls.

Then it was his turn to speak. "I'm from Philadelphia."

"Yo, Philly."

"No. Nobody in Philly calls it 'Philly' except people who aren't from there. It's 'Philadelphia.'" That wasn't entirely true, but he liked the idea of messing with him. "And as far as being in Hungary, well I ain't really seen shit yet."

Some of the others nodded in assent.

"You'll get your chance," Doornail said. "How 'bout you?" he asked another man. "Where you from, soldier?"

The conversation went on like that, and they hung on every word. Doornail took tiny sips from the whiskey and pretended to get tipsy. Once they went around the whole group, he riled them with stories about the titty bars in Budapest and the hot-blooded Hungarian girls. "God*damn!* Springtime in Budapest is a glorious sight! Play your cards right, toe the line, and I bet your man Sullivan'll hook you up with a pass to come visit."

The other soldiers bought the fake camaraderie like a five-dollar blowjob. One of them asked Doornail how he got the name.

"Back in O-Town . . . I mean, Oakland," he said, looking at Brutus. "I got it when I was a teenager, and it just stuck." He practiced his little laugh. "When I was sixteen I moved into my own crib. Sure, O-Town had a bad rep, but I never felt endangered in any way until then. I get there and I can tell right away that some of the folks in the hood were waiting to fuck with me."

The word "fuck" sounded funny coming from him, like when an American solider spent too much time with the few remaining Brits and started saying shit like "bloody" and "wanker."

"It's a predatory thing in Oakland, and I was the new kid. Like you men here."

Brutus paid a little more attention. He watched Doornail's eyes as he spoke, but he couldn't get any read.

"Day I move in, I pick up this dead rat out back. Big sucker. And I nail it to my front door, *bam bam bam.* I wanted to send a message to the neighborhood. You know, don't fuck with me. Sure enough, I get up next morning and the rat's gone. Somebody came up and stole it right off my door. Now this is a tough neighborhood! But you know what? No one messed with me after that. People didn't shy away. I mean, they couldn't let me be a badass by crucifying a rat on my door, but they didn't mess with me neither."

When the staff sergeant knocked on the door, everyone stood to shake Doornail's hand. "Next time, I'll see you men up in the city," he told them, and exited like a rock star.

2.

Brutus picked up the Fanon book and then put it back down in frustration. The unorthodox visit from the marines was little more than another thinly veiled threat, a demonstration of Sullivan's far-reaching influence, of the width and breadth of his might. Army life consisted of continuing battles of the will and the establishment of petty superiorities over one's fellow man. He witnessed the ill-natured competitiveness most often in the mess hall and on the shooting ranges. Sullivan was the reigning champion of the big-dick contests, none of which had been mentioned at the recruiter's office on Broad Street, under the gaze of that Quaker-ass William Penn.

The constant threat of terrorist attacks on American targets at home and abroad required Brutus to carry his firearm at all times, and his needed a good cleaning. The army was training the goddamn Iraqi police there on the base. That was what they called it. "Training" them in the fine art of torture, to be sure. Private jets landed every couple of days on an airstrip built specifically for the base's restricted zone.

Doornail's story stayed with him longer than he would have preferred. The image of the dead rat lingered on the periphery of Brutus's thoughts, slightly out of focus but vivid enough to unsettle everything around it. There was a lesson in it—something foreboding, but he couldn't put his finger on it. He was taking apart his weapon when someone banged on his door. He didn't answer it, but the knock came again. "Private First Class Gibson? You're to report to Sullivan's office immediately."

Probably just a couple knuckleheads busting his balls.

"Hold up." He clanged the pieces of his pistol together loud enough that they wouldn't think he was jerking off.

A pair of Latino soldiers stood in the doorway, sending an elongated, fun-house shadow into his room. An open window backlit their helmets like two metallic haloes—a carefully cultivated effect. Brutus made a show of keeping his hands out in the open. He had grown suspicious of cops long before his arrival in Europe.

"You Gibson?"

"Yeah."

One of the soldiers shifted his weight, sending a blinding light directly into Brutus's eyes and rendering himself invisible. "Sullivan wants to see you."

"Right now?" He looked back at the row of metal that had recently been a pistol. Regulations forbade him from leaving without it. He could go to jail for having an unsecured weapon in a barracks room.

"No, when your gold-plated invitation arrives," the other guy said.

The authorities there were just as witty in Budapest as they were in Philly.

"Hold up."

Brutus considered putting the pistol back together first but decided to forget it. He grabbed his wallet from his desk and followed the M.P.s out, pulling the door locked behind him. A dozen minor infractions of protocol committed over the past few days came to mind, none of which warranted a personal summons from Sullivan.

Brutus refused to be the first to speak. He allowed the cops to feel that they had adequately established their authority. Unfortunately, they weren't just fronting—he really *was* more or less at their mercy. There were all kinds of stories about out-of-uniform soldiers dragging men from their rooms, taking them behind the latrines, and treating them like Rodney King for a day. Brutus wasn't about to make the first move.

Sullivan's office was over in the executive suite of newer buildings on the western edge of the camp. Brutus's sometime-girlfriend, a civilian named Magda, occasionally worked there as an interpreter. She spent most of her time in the restricted area, and wouldn't talk about what went on there. He couldn't even bring up the topic. The cops directed him into the back of a Humvee, which slid on the ice around the turns. Other soldiers watched without surprise as the three of them passed. Brutus read their eyes: he had had this coming for a long time.

Lieutenant Colonel Sullivan sat smiling behind his desk. Brutus had never even spoken to him, other than "yes" and "sir." This ought to be good, he thought. He saluted and stood at attention. "Private First Class Jonathan Gibson reporting as ordered, sir."

Up close, Sullivan appeared cross-eyed; he had the lazy eye of a sniper who had spent too many hours staring down the scope of a rifle either out in the field or from the roof of an embassy someplace. His bright green eyes glowed in violent contrast to the taut, ruddy complexion of his skin. A framed blueprint of a small military bridge occupied the entire wall behind him. Sullivan had overseen its reconstruction over a river in Serbia and was awarded a commendation from the highest echelons of SFOR. Young for a man of his rank, he had a reputation as a cunning, brutal officer. He was the biggest ballbreaker on the continent. It was said that his assignment to Hungary was a form of punishment, or possibly even exile. A soldier in his command had once died under allegedly crooked circumstances. Brutus had to stay sharp. Smile and nod.

"At ease," Sullivan said. "Relax, Brutus." His voice was calming in an authoritative way, kind of like how they portrayed Satan's in old movies. Brutus remained standing. Sullivan saw the surprise on his face. "You don't mind if I call you Brutus, do you?"

"No, sir."

Sullivan dismissed the soldiers. He had a large manila envelope on the desk. The words PFC GIBSON JONATHAN and PHILADELPHIA, PENNA. were typed on a white label.

"Do you know why you're here?"

"No, sir." A million possibilities ran through his mind. They probably knew about Magda. Relations with the civilian population had been forbidden since another G.I. got convicted of rape in Japan some months earlier and set off a diplomatic shitstorm. Word had it that parents in Okinawa, probably in Hungary too, were trying to cash in on the American occupation by sending their daughters out to fuck soldiers and then yell rape. Uncle Sam was known to throw a lot of money around to keep the stories out of the papers. At Taszár, the authorities didn't care if a G.I. poked another Hungarian honey, not until they needed an excuse to climb up his ass.

Sullivan slid the envelope across the desk. Brutus became aware not only of his own nervousness but also how much Sullivan relished that nervousness. He bathed in it, took strength from it. He was probably stroking a hard-on under his desk. He looked like a snake about to lunge at a rat. A thought ran through Brutus's mind: a snake without poison is still a snake. He couldn't remember where he'd heard that. Maybe from his buddy Elvin. He opened the envelope, which was empty except for a single eight-by-ten photo.

"Look at the photograph, Private."

It was black-and-white and extremely grainy, with a spooky, timeless quality. It could have been taken twenty minutes or twenty years earlier: a hard-core shot of two men, one black and one white, engaging in anal sex. From the angle and quality of the print, he couldn't make out either of their faces. The black man was getting fucked up the ass, and Brutus knew what was going to happen next.

"What's the matter, Brutus? That is you, isn't it? That nigger faggot, I mean." All the softness left his voice. A thin smile crept across his face.

"No, sir."

"Do you always catch, Brutus? Don't you get the urge to pitch once in a while?" Sullivan stopped smiling. "Listen to me. This is you in the photograph. Do you understand?"

"Sir, I—"

"Do. You. Under. Stand?"

Brutus looked deep into Sullivan's face and saw nothing at all he could work with. His mind raced. A snake without poison is still a snake. It wasn't him in the photo, of course, but that would be his word against Sullivan's. How many men had Sullivan pulled this on? How many different people had been in that picture? Did he have another version with the roles reversed in the unlikely case that he wanted to blackmail a white dude? A Latino? Sullivan was setting him up. Blackmail—the word rolled over and over through his mind. He entertained the idea that the white guy in the photo was Sullivan.

"Yes, sir. I understand."

Brutus *did* understand. For the first time in his army career, he knew exactly what was happening to him. He was being set up, made into an example at Taszár and at every post Sullivan would have for the remainder of his career.

"You see that it's you in the photograph?"

"Yes, sir."

"It pleases me to know you're as smart as our best testing demonstrates. So you understand that you have officially entered into a world of shit? So to speak."

"Very much so, sir."

"And, Private, that I alone can get you out of it?"

"I pretty much guessed that too, sir. And if I'm not mistaken you're going to make me some kind of deal." Brutus sidestepped the usual formalities, testing his limits. He wished he had his pistol with him, but didn't know what he would do with it. Better this way.

"You're perceptive, Private. But this is not the time to discuss such matters. For now, let's just say that you are going to help me with something. When you're finished, you get to keep this photograph as a souvenir. Fuck with me, and this is going on the front page of *Stars and Stripes*. You get where I'm coming from?"

"Yes, sir."

"You won't end up in some cushy, American prison. Oh no. It would please me very much to visit you in the filthiest cell this whole stinking country has to offer, and I will blow you sweet kisses while you're bent over in front of some skinhead mother killers far meaner than the featherweight in this picture. Dismissed, Private."

Brutus saluted and turned to leave.

"Oh, one more thing before you go, Private. With a name like Brutus, I assume you've read *Julius Caesar*?"

"Yes, sir. Several times, sir." He even had "Et tu Brute" tattooed on his left bicep.

"Well. A nigger who reads Shakespeare is like the one monkey out of a thousand that gets lucky at a typewriter and writes a sonnet. That makes you one lucky monkey, doesn't it?"

"Yes, sir."

"So when I tell you to beware the ides of March, you know you better fucking listen, right?"

"Yes, sir." Brutus couldn't stand the sound of his own voice: yessuh, yessuh, yessuh. "But it wasn't Brutus, sir."

The lieutenant colonel looked up from the paperwork on his desk. "Excuse me?"

"It wasn't Brutus, sir, who had to beware the ides of March. It was Caesar."

Sullivan scowled. "Dismissed, Private."

3.

"This is *not,*" Sullivan had announced in his introductory lecture, "a free country."

The day Brutus had arrived at Taszár, he received an orientation package of army propaganda. More than national defense or fighting wars or peacekeeping missions or any of that, *paperwork* justified the existence of the U.S. military. He was handed three three-ring binders stacked one on top of the other. That was only the beginning. He pitched most of the material into the garbage, but kept a few pamphlets because of their comic value. One described the dangers of Hungarian women, known to be a predatory race of acid-tongued nymphets interested only in obtaining an American passport. There was nothing a Hungarian girl—especially "a girl from the countryside," it was stressed—wouldn't do to sink her claws into a G.I. The handout told horror stories of girls getting pregnant and demanding child support from the U.S. government, of angry fathers seeking retribution ("The honor of one's family is extremely important among the peasantry of Eastern Europe"), and of mafioso thugs using their girlfriends as bait to extort money out of the unwitting soldier. "Socially Transmitted Diseases (STDs) run rampant in emerging democracies."

The battery of physical and psychological examinations, and the innumerable injections, lasted for weeks.

Back before the construction of Camp Bondsteel over in Kosovo, the American brass decided that Taszár Air Base could be another

Guantánamo. Originally built for the Red Army in the 1950s, it was conveniently located within striking distance of the Yugoslavian border. The Russians abandoned the base in 1990 and a few years later, Uncle Sam moved in. To the Hungarian government, opening Taszár to the United States gave them a jackbooted foot in the door to NATO. The Budapest media, like the American, was effectively state run and did little to feed the nation's appetite for political scandal, even in the face of another occupation by another imperial power.

Taszár served for a short time as the operational headquarters for the theoretically multinational force charged with "keeping the peace" in the Balkans. Once things cooled down over there, though, the American government refused to decommission the base. Instead, they repurposed it for use in their War on Terror. It wasn't like they could illegally intern civilians on American soil—they had tried that with the Japanese during World War II—so instead, they used bases like Taszár. The so-called black sites. The few Brits and Dutchmen Brutus saw around existed purely for symbolic purposes. For obvious historical reasons, there were very few Russian, or even German, soldiers on Hungarian soil.

Brutus rarely had any contact with the foreign troops or with the few Hungarian officers who, in theory, still technically ran the base. He knew the deal. His presence at Taszár represented another step in Hungary's transition from Soviet satellite state to American satellite state. No one in the army appeared willing to question the exportation of America's racist, imperialist tradition into yet another foreign land. Most of the other soldiers, even the rare black officer, couldn't distinguish between Eldridge and Beaver Cleaver.

The whole base reminded Brutus of Eastern State Penitentiary back home. That was the first real prison built in the colonies, but it hadn't housed prisoners for at least thirty years. He had taken a tour there once with his sister, before she had J. J. The administrators opened it to the public in summertime and at Halloween turned it into a haunted house. Sometimes one of the local universities would rent it out to put on plays and shit, but the theatergoers had to wear hardhats because the place was in such dismal shape. The prison was designed so that a guard in a central tower could see into every cell. It didn't matter if you were being watched at any given time—you had to behave because you knew you *could* be being watched.

Taszár worked in the same, panoptic way. The army created a pervasive environment of paranoia. There was one notable difference, though. Instead of just the officers and the M.P.s being able to see everything going on all the time, all of the soldiers—like the prisoners they were—could as well. Everyone knew everyone else's intimate business. If someone stole food from the mess hall, or snuck across the motor pool to play a little grab-ass with one of the Hungarian civilians, everyone knew about it. The testosterone-powered cycle trapped everyone on the base in a feedback loop of constant surveillance. That included the foreign troops too. The M.P.s didn't even need to keep an eye on the soldiers. They policed themselves and each other, just like Orwell had predicted. Even if Brutus *wasn't* being watched at any given time, the police and Sparky and these other hillbillies *could be* watching him, and that was usually enough to make him think twice about doing something stupid. His letters from home were read, his e-mails intercepted, and his uppity behavior reported, all in the name of national security. But hanging out with Magda on occasion was the one bright spot in the dreary grind of army life. He heard the racist murmurings behind his back about his dating a white woman, sure, and although no one said much to his face, there existed a constant threat of reprisal from some gung-ho supremacist.

He felt the weight of his pistol bouncing against his hip with each step. Its presence unsettled him not because he didn't want to carry it, but because he didn't like the fact that everyone else was carrying a weapon too. There were too many cowboys running around, anxious to lay down their own personal versions of the law. The higher-ups readily encouraged a system of justice that wasn't based upon any consistent moral authority Brutus could identify. What, in his reading, Paul Ricoeur referred to as "the practical field" Brutus thought of as "the Man." And at Taszár, each man had become the Man to the other men. Himself included.

When someone got caught fucking up, it was only elevated to the M.P.s if the situation—and the punishment—couldn't be handled first within the ranks. As a message, a solider might get stuck on shithole duty for a month, or even pistol-whipped while he slept. The inmates ran the jail, which was why it was so dangerous not only letting everyone run around with a firearm but *requiring* it. West Philly had been the same back in the eighties, when everyone carried a piece because of all the crackheads. There were shoot-outs every night. Elvin got himself shot in the stomach and had a scar from his ribs all the way down his fat belly.

Apart from catching up with Magda now and then, Brutus stayed more or less in line. He sometimes voiced his more subversive political views, but still, he never expected this kind of trouble, least of all from Sullivan and the higher-ups.

Being watched and scrutinized all the time was bad enough, but the people watching him were now better armed than he was. His weapon no longer functioned properly and hadn't for a few days, since a couple of components got lost the day he left it in his room to go see Sullivan. Huge disadvantage. And he couldn't just go and order replacement parts either. Questions would be asked, discipline administered. Fuck all that.

He suspected that Sparky found the pieces and dumped them down the toilet. Brutus was already in a world of trouble, though, so he didn't care if his roommate put the word out, as he invariably would, that his sidearm didn't shoot. He carried it with him anyway. Like all things in the army, his weapon existed for the sake of appearance. Every day, he regretted quitting college. Every single fucking day.

Brutus had attended Temple University for two years, where he studied philosophy and took computer classes, but he found he learned more on his own, reading whatever he wanted. He dropped out and took a job as a security guard at the Macy's next to city hall, which everyone still called Wanamaker's. Every day, on the bus ride to the store, he passed the recruiter's office. At the Mambo's urging he went in and, desperate to hear some good news, believed every last lie they sold him. Money for college, if he ever decided to go back. Rapid advancement. No color barrier. On-the-job training. See the world, hold your chin high, become a man. Nothing at all about the army maintaining the last vestiges of the American slave trade.

He signed on. By week three of basic training, the Seven Army Values felt like deadly sins, and he knew he had made a mistake. The limited potential for career growth afforded an inner-city brother in the U.S. Army soon became clear. They made no attempt to pretend otherwise. Now punks like Sparky dirtied their lily-white hands on ink-jet printouts while Brutus stood out in the freezing cold setting rattraps. The local rodents carried a virus that had made several soldiers sick. Brutus had personally baited over a hundred traps, but to date had caught only nine rats. The men who sucked up to Sullivan didn't necessarily rise any quicker through the ranks, but they did get the sweetest assignments. Sparky sat in ops reading satellite images or monitoring Radio Beograd while Brutus and the other brothers and Latinos caught vermin in the snow or broke up the ice that formed every night on the runway.

Contrary to the propagandists' advice, Brutus didn't fear the wrath of Hungarian women and their social diseases. He had been seeing Magda for the past two months. Conjugal relations with members of the civilian crews were expressly forbidden, but when Magda could sneak loose Brutus arranged to meet her someplace quiet. To do so, he needed to cut across the base to get to the prefab buildings where the officers ran their war. In the army, Brutus had learned, if he acted like he belonged in a certain situation, no one would question him. He could do anything he wanted to so long as he did it with a little authority. Put that glide in his stride and he could probably saunter back into Sullivan's office and wet him on the spot. If his pistol worked.

In the absence of wind, a three-foot-tall cloud of truck exhaust lingered just off the ground. He followed it to Sullivan's building. Odors didn't dissipate in that weather, so the entire base smelled like oil and gunpowder, plus cooking grease and fresh paint. His sinuses were so blocked that the stink didn't bother him as much as usual. He blew his nose, filling a tissue with soot and tar that looked like the resin coating the inside of a glass pipe. Then the oily smell hit him, only for a second, until his nose clogged up again.

Someone had used a cinder block to prop open a back door. A dozen cigarette butts lay crushed on the ground. Brutus slipped inside and, as planned, found Magda in an otherwise unoccupied meeting room.

She was maybe a decade older than him but didn't show it, and she spoke half a dozen languages. Her father was Hungarian, and although Magda grew up in America and went to Yale, Brutus thought of her as Hungarian. She was real cool, not as materialistic as most of the women he knew back home, even though he got the impression she was pretty well-off. She worked as a translator or a consultant or something like that. It was classified. She was also gorgeous, with the kind of smile that made army life and the rest of the world disappear.

It was said that after Attila the Hun conquered all of Central and Eastern Europe he rounded up the most beautiful women in his empire and set up his personal harem in what would later become Hungary. That was why Hungarian girls were so hot and why they differed so much in appearance. On the cleaning crews alone, Brutus saw girls with olive, Latin features, girls with Viking-blonde hair and blue eyes, and even girls with round faces and Asian-looking eyes. Magda had black curly hair and ruby lips. She was also five times smarter than anyone he had ever met.

He closed the door tight by jamming a wooden chair under the handle. She spilled all over him. Magda took off her clothes and underneath she had on her usual G-string panties, which he didn't bother to remove. She obviously worked out, because she was strong for a woman and not at all averse to fighting back here and there. She had a nasty streak in her. They played rough. Brutus wondered if she had ever zapped an Arab with a cattle prod. She wore this expensive perfume she had had specially made in Dubai and as she rubbed against him, it rose from her skin. It smelled like fresh leather that had been treated with rose water and licorice. It drove him crazy.

After, as they got dressed, someone rapped at the door. "Halló?" a voice called out. It belonged to the head of the cleaning crew, a round old troll who, much to the amusement of the girls in her command, barked at Brutus in Hungarian whenever she saw him.

"Egy pillanat!" Magda told her.

Brutus gave the troll ten bucks to keep her quiet. That was a ton of money to some old lady making maybe two hundred dollars a month, and he didn't have anything to spend it on anyway, except fast food and those bullshit Tom Clancy novels. Magda kissed him and went back to work. Before he left, he waited a few minutes to catch his breath and to allow any passersby to disappear.

He decided to put off rattrap duty and return to his room, Magda's perfume still clinging to his body. Sparky was out. The image Sullivan had showed him remained burned onto his brain, like spots after staring at the sun. Brutus felt like he *had* been fucked up the ass. It was the fifth of March. Ten days until whatever Sullivan had planned. That didn't give Brutus a ton of time to get his shit together.

Brutus put on some Public Enemy and yanked open his closet door. He threw all his clothes onto the bed, then pulled open the drawers of his dresser and dumped the contents onto the pile. Taking a pair of nail scissors from his desk, he poked it through the heart of a brand-new shirt that the Mambo had sent him for Christmas. Cutting a crude circle through the breast, he ripped the Polo insignia out and dropped the rough swatch of cloth onto the floor. Picking up the next shirt, he did the same thing. He repeated the process with every article of clothing he owned, tearing out all the corporate symbols, insignias, and logos. They were the trademarks of the white devil, of Satan himself. One after another, he stripped the tags off the pockets of his Levi's and cut the swooshes out of his socks, until a stack of capitalist-propaganda cotton lay at his feet like broken shackles. He would have loved nothing more than to rip the U.S. ARMY patches off his uniforms, but he couldn't go there. Not yet.

Next, he carefully refolded his T-shirts and socks, and replaced his dress shirts and pants in the closet. He picked up the discarded patches and put them in a manila envelope, like the one on Sullivan's desk. He addressed it to his sister and included a note on a three-by-five card: "Please use these to make me a quilt."

He put the card in the envelope, but before sealing it pulled it out again. He erased "quilt" and wrote "flag" instead. It would take ten days to get to her.

4.

Sparky was listening to a Hungarian pop station that played terrible American eighties music interspersed with heavily orchestrated Hungarian headbanger ballads while surfing the net for porn on a signed-out laptop. He lifted his chin in hello and turned the screen to face Brutus, who leaned over his roommate's shoulder to see an image of two heavily tattooed men dressed up like pizza delivery boys penetrating different ends of the same surgically augmented woman. The elaborate set looked like the living room of a mansion, with a roaring fireplace and a bearskin rug. She was lying on her stomach on a glass coffee table and still had on her high heels. Two thick art books had been kicked to the floor. Brutus couldn't make out the titles. Sparky, who had a way with words, said, "Looks like fun, doesn't it?"

The image reminded Brutus of the photo on Sullivan's desk. "What do you bother with that shit for? Big pretty man like you, I bet you get more tang than Buzz Aldrin."

"Everyone says you're the one tagging that Magda bitch. Every guy in camp's been trying to get in her pants."

Brutus shrugged. "I can neither confirm nor deny those charges. Besides, what's a punk like you care about a hottie like Magda anyway?"

"Fuck you."

"Good comeback."

"O.K., fuck you, Shakespeare."

Even Brutus had to laugh—but he didn't care for the allusion. What if Sparky was in on the blackmail? Unlikely, but not impossible. Sullivan was *not* the kind of man to leave a roommate assignment to chance. Brutus couldn't trust anybody.

He removed his hat, coat, and boots, then he turned the heater down a notch and finally sat. His feet were killing him. Commotion filled the hallway outside. Someone was barking like a dog. He flipped on his desk lamp, which provided a nasty, halogen glow. He opened his journal, a hardbound art-school sketchbook Joan had given him as a going-away gift. The edges were painted a shiny biblical gold, and Brutus had titled it "The Myth of Syphilis" in neat block letters on the flyleaf. He filled one page every day even when he had nothing new to say. He kept the book in his underwear drawer. Sparky knew of its existence, which meant that everyone knew of its existence, but there was nothing Brutus could do about that. As a general rule, he tried to limit his worries to those things he could control. There weren't many in the army.

He stood again and pulled a half-liter bottle of Dreher from the little dorm fridge they shared. The P.X. sold American beer, but Brutus would have his whole life left to drink that shit when he got home, and at least the Hungarian stuff had some flavor to it. The cold, uncarpeted floor stung his feet. Back at his desk, he tried to clear his head, think things through. The beer brought a flush to his cheeks.

One week—that was how much time he had. Sullivan was probably running smack or something up from the Croatian coast. Brutus knew from personal experience about the Croats' well-earned reputation for producing high-quality pharmaceuticals. It must have been something about the weather down there. Magda had gotten her hands on some serious, not-to-be-fucked-with shit. The Adriatic kind bud was as good as the best bubonic chronic that ever crossed through Philly. Brutus grew up smoking weed the way redneck kids grew up slurping Mountain Dew. His old man knew every reggae band that came through town, and they would come around to see him. He used to jam with some of those guys back in Kingston, but sold his bass when he got married and moved to the States. Brutus would get up on Sunday morning and Bunny or Toots or someone would be sitting on the front porch rolling a fatty. The Mambo would be irate about it all day. Every Sunday she would make a huge pot of curried goat to last the week, and most of the time the old man and his friends would kill it before it got dark. She wasn't crazy about having all that weed around either, and that may have been part of the reason she kicked the old man out. Brutus currently had half an ounce stashed in a sock, but there was no way he could light up with Sparky in the room. Maybe he *was* getting paranoid, like Joan always said, but he was already in enough trouble.

Carrying drugs for Sullivan would be no joke. He had singled Brutus out to make an example of him, to cure the Uppity Negro Syndrome before it could spread and contaminate the rest of the base. Don't ask, don't tell. Turn the other cheek in the army and you ended up with a dick in your ass. Taszár had its share of drug addicts and every variety of alcoholic. Whoring. Hookers would show up by the carload, each carrying a bottle of home-brewed pálinka and a toothbrush. The M.P.s sometimes accepted kickbacks to look the other way, or got a piece for themselves.

Independent thought, on the other hand—that was the biggest sin of them all. The *only* sin in the army. And independent thought from a black man was even worse. So Sullivan decided to use him as a scapegoat. He ran the base like an old Southern cracker running his plantation. He had his field niggers, like Brutus, who did the hard work—digging holes and lugging bags of concrete and shit. Then there were the house niggers, like that marine punk Doornail and the M.P.s, the adopted love children of the gay union of Uncle Sam and Uncle Tom.

Before that meeting with Sullivan, the only time Brutus had ever been officially reprimanded was the time he wrote a letter home to the *Philadelphia Inquirer* about some Supreme Court opinion by Clarence Thomas that he had read about online. Brutus had referred to the current administration as "Uncle Tom's Cabinet," and made a comment about how Ruth Bader Ginsburg and "all those other white Washington bitches" had better look out. He concluded with something about Amiri being right about 9/11. They didn't print the word "bitches" in the paper, but the message came across all the same. The recruiter back on Broad Street, the old bastard who had suckered Brutus in the first place, saw the letter and sent a copy to Sullivan. As punishment, Brutus was confined to the base for twelve months.

He tapped his pen on the cover of his journal until Sparky got annoyed, then kept doing it. If it wasn't running drugs, what else?

Weapons were a possibility, but everyone already owned guns in Eastern Europe. They had more guns than they could use. Wasn't a soul left who needed to buy guns from the army—with the possible exception of Brutus himself, who was still without a working firearm. Maybe someone over in the restricted camp was picking up some supplies on the down-low, cattle prods and waterboards and shit—and providing Sullivan with a taste of the action.

The whole thing could go down like this: Sullivan will send Brutus off the base, placing him at an even greater disadvantage because suddenly he would no longer be just a sodomite but also AWOL. While he's away, Sullivan will drop a couple keys of coke in Brutus's top dresser drawer, call in the pigs, and have his ass thrown in the pen. Hungary had fucked-up drug laws, the harshest of any non-Muslim country, all intended as a suck up to NATO and the E.U. If Brutus got nabbed with as much as a pin-prick of resin in the bottom of a pipe, it would mean a *minimum* of a year in jail.

Sparky switched off the radio and headed out, so Brutus turned it on again and put in Fela Kuti's *Expensive Shit*.

More likely than not, though, Sullivan probably planned to simply send him on some goose chase intended to frighten him into becoming a model soldier. Scare him straight. Instill in him the fear of God and of his earthly incarnation, Uncle Sam. Brutus would get his delinquent ass kicked, caught with drugs or something, and be given the ultimatum: toe the line, quit the political bullshit, and Sullivan will make all his problems disappear, including the photograph. What a guy.

Brutus wrote the date at the top of the page. Under it, he made a to-do list:

1. Reread *Julius Caesar*

They might have a copy at the P.X.

2. Write letter to Mom

Later. He couldn't even think about that yet. What was he going to say? "Dear Mambo, My commanding officer has a picture of me getting fucked up the ass so I have to go buy some drugs for him. Love, B." Doubtful.

3. Write letter to Joan

He wanted to tell his sister the whole story, start to finish. And then he would get Magda to mail it for him, in case Sullivan was going through the mail. Couldn't be too careful. The army could open a letter without anyone knowing the envelope had been touched by human hands, read the contents, and rewrite it on the same type of stationery in the same handwriting. Signature and everything. Brutus wrote it all down for Joan, including the conversation with Sullivan, and hid it in an envelope from one of her letters.

4. Write letter to J. J.

Another tough one—later.

5. Fix pistol or find new

6. Kill whitey

He had about three grand in cash, which would go with him. The weapon wouldn't be a problem. He could steal Sparky's and leave him the piece-of-shit piece that didn't shoot. Punk deserved it anyway.

Number six was a joke.

5.

When he got up the next morning, snow covered the ground and was blowing in every direction. He didn't need to be on duty until the afternoon and he wasn't hungry, so he skipped breakfast to run some errands. He could grab something later if he got desperate, but he hated to eat the hardened fecal matter that passed for meat at those fast-food places. Burger King was terrible enough back home; he didn't even want to think about what went into the Hungarian equivalent of the Whopper. Maybe that's what his rattraps were for. But sometimes there was no avoiding it. A man's got to eat.

He pulled his jacket tighter, huffing it over to the office pool. When he was sure no one was looking, he whipped his dick out of his fatigues. Standing on tiptoe, he put it on the glass of the machine, set the enlarger to 150 percent and hit COPY. Zipping up, he folded the image and, laughing, stuffed it into another envelope. Back in his room, there was no safe place to hide anything, so he put the photocopy and the letter to Joan in Sparky's closet between a few old boxes. There was a good chance his own stuff was being searched, maybe even by his own roommate. In Sparky's possession, though, at least no one would find them in the next few days.

His next stop was Taszár's small bookstore of government-approved texts, which operated under the auspices of a university in Budapest that served as the personal propaganda ministry of a well-known Hungarian billionaire war profiteer. They didn't have a copy of *Julius Caesar*. He would have liked to bring Magda some poetry, but she had already read *everything*, and all they had for sale was that old Emily Dickinson shit. "Stop for death, my ass," Brutus told the clerk, a lanky, bucktoothed Hungarian girl of fifteen or sixteen. She didn't respond. The shop had nothing worth buying, so Brutus left without spending any money, a noble accomplishment. He didn't like the idea of giving any more of his money to the army than he had to. Didn't want to sell his soul to no Bravo Company store.

The base was unusually busy. Transports rolled out one after the other for either bridge-building duty in Novi Sad or to oversee still more landmine sweeping in Kosovo. All the trucks had SFOR stenciled on them in bright blue letters. A couple of them carried soldiers up to Budapest for R and R. The army reserved countless hotel suites along the Danube for years at a time. One of the hotels supposedly had thermal baths in the basement where all the women bathed together naked. That sounded like a damn good way to relax.

He was anxious to see Magda. It had been a few days. He wanted to question her about Sullivan, see if she had overheard anything. He went in through the back door and poked around, but couldn't find her. A few officers looked at him funny, but he saluted and pretended he was supposed to be there. He wasn't *supposed* to be anywhere in the whole goddamned country so the executive suite was just as good as anyplace else. Magda wasn't around. The fifteenth was still a few days away, so he had some time before giving her the letter to mail home.

He returned the next day, let himself in again, and finally caught up with her. She looked great, her hair down at her shoulders instead of all tied up in knots and loops, like it usually was. She didn't have any makeup on and it was the first time Brutus had ever gotten a look at her full, natural splendor. She had bright eyes that floated like lily pads when they looked at him. No perfume this time either, which he found strange.

The bosses must have been up her ass because she couldn't get away. "*Not* a good time," she said. "Let's catch up later." She didn't want to be seen talking with him. She worked for a private civilian contractor, though, so it wasn't like they could throw her in the stockade.

"That's cool, but here," he said, and handed Magda an envelope with her name on it. Inside was another envelope addressed to his sister. She slipped it into her pocket without opening it and kissed him on the lips.

"See you tomorrow?" she wanted to know.

"Yeah, tomorrow's good."

She kissed him again, a half second longer, and headed off in the direction of Sullivan's office. Brutus returned to his room to prepare for afternoon rattrap duty, which meant cracking open a Dreher and rolling up a blunt.

Work was more tedious than difficult, and he had trouble concentrating. Still too much to do before the fifteenth. Afterwards, he took a shower and tried to empty his thoughts of his responsibilities and duties.

He wrote a letter to the Mambo about nothing in particular. She could get the details from Joan. He told her that he loved her and would be home soon. Then he lay down to read from the Fanon book, and to get some rest. By the time sleep came, he had agreed to let events take him wherever they wanted to. He would follow whatever path presented itself. This was his life; he could feel it.

He awoke refreshed and ate a large, flavorless breakfast. It was the fourteenth. He didn't need to be on duty until 16:00, so he went to check on Magda. As fate would have it—or luck, for that matter, which to Brutus looked like fate in a cheap wig and bad shoes—she was thrilled to see him. She was heavily made-up again, much to his disappointment, but that didn't detract from her beauty. She kissed him hard, and he tasted the oily surface of her tongue in his mouth, got the first whiff of her perfume. She agreed to sneak off with him.

In the best-case scenario, he would only be off the base for a day. Two at the most. Magda never needed to know he was gone. He didn't want to get her mixed up in whatever Sullivan was playing at.

The worst-case scenario was something Brutus tried to put out of his mind.

He followed Magda to a conference room just a few doors down from Sullivan's office. She clearly knew her way around. A meeting had recently broken up probably, or the generals were taking a break from planning how to kill more people: their files and half-empty coffee cups were strewn everywhere. Overflowing manila folders covered the long conference table with briefings, some of which must have been highly classified. They could come back any second, and the possibility of getting busted either didn't occur to Magda or it excited her even more. What would they do if they caught him? It didn't matter anymore. White dry-erase boards covered two whole walls with crudely illustrated maps of the Balkans. The national boundaries had been drawn and redrawn in several places on both maps, each time with a different colored marker. On the table, a laptop remained on. The screensaver read I'D RATHER BE FUCKING YOUR MOTHER in scrolling text.

Brutus didn't bother to lock the door. There was nothing left to lose anymore. He pushed the computer aside, lifted Magda onto the edge of the table, and pulled up her skirt. She had on a pair of sexy see-through panties, like she had been waiting for him. Her perfume billowed off of her neck and chest—it was enough to make him want to spend the rest of his life writing love songs for her. She grabbed him closer, rubbing up against him and breathing in his ear until he couldn't hear anything else. He knew someone was about to fly through the door any minute and wondered if Magda would yell rape just to save her own job. But he didn't stop. Papers fell to the floor in piles. She kicked at the maps on the whiteboards, further blurring the Serbia-Bosnia border. When she stopped huffing and the blood no longer pounded in his head, Brutus noticed that a shortwave radio on a bookshelf had been playing the entire time. Magda recomposed herself, getting dressed and fixing her hair in the reflection of the laptop's screen while Armed Forces Radio bleated the current number-one song, a bastardization of Billie's "Strange Fruit," to which someone had added a gaudy drum-and-bass rhythm.

Brutus zipped up, then sat in a cushy office chair at the head of the table and pulled Magda to him again.

"Oh, no," she said. "I need to get back."

He didn't release her. A part of him was in love with Magda. When the time came, maybe he would invite her to visit him in Philly. But that was too far down the road to even contemplate. And imagine what Elvin would say when Brutus showed up around the block with a rich white woman on his arm. He could already hear the abuse he would get.

Before she could wiggle away, he handed her a small bundle of letters he needed mailed. Three of them contained the whole truth and were addressed to media outlets and a congresswoman in Philly, and a fourth was made out to Sullivan care of the base. The last one contained the anonymous photocopied enlargement of his penis. Brutus smacked Magda on the backside and let her go.

6.

The pigs rarely enforced lights-out so Brutus kept his desk lamp on. Sparky grumbled about it but was too much of a chickenshit to say anything; he was clearly Sullivan's stooge, if not his outright bitch. Brutus watched the clock. He would need some rest, but there was no goddamn way he would be able to sleep. The phone was going to ring or the door would open just wide enough for some corrupt M.P. to shine a flashlight in his eyes. He stayed in bed reading.

Midnight came and went: it became the ides of March.

The clock hands crawled toward morning. Brutus no longer cared what happened so long as it happened soon. Now. Every so often he felt like he might have fallen asleep for a minute or two. The clock stared back at him.

At least he was a step ahead of Sullivan, and he took some small satisfaction from that. He had purchased a prepaid phone card from the P.X. and called ahead to the Vienna Hilton to book a room under his own name. He left a map of that city in his desk, where Sparky was certain to sniff it out. Sullivan's people would look for him in Austria, which just might provide enough diversion to buy some extra time if he needed to haul ass out of the country to Slovakia, or even to Serbia. Getting over the border would be difficult without his passport, but not impossible. All G.I.s at Taszár were required to surrender their papers to their commanding officers upon arriving, which was just as good as having a leash around the neck that reached all the way to Hungary's borders, but not a step further, like the dog in the cartoons.

Brutus hid thin bundles of twenty-, fifty-, and one-hundred-dollar bills in the lining of his jacket and wrapped two changes of clothes—one military, one civilian—in separate plastic bags. The civvies had those holes cut out of them, making them a little more conspicuous, but he didn't care. It would be better than wearing the trademarked signs of the devil. Might as well wear chains like his homies back home enslaving themselves in collars of thick gold bling.

If returning to Taszár didn't turn out to be an option, he might very well end up either in jail or with a dog tag around his toe. He didn't spend the time contemplating which would be worse. If he had to, he could beep Elvin and some people back home and get them to call Channel 6 Action News. All the info they'd need was in the letters Magda mailed, so he just needed to stay alive and out of jail long enough to get some backup.

When the door finally opened, Brutus pretended to be asleep. A single set of footsteps approached his bunk. Sparky was also awake. Brutus steadied himself for a shot to the ribs, but it didn't come. The bed sagged as a duffel bag landed on the blankets next to his feet. It was heavy. Black steel in the hour of chaos. He didn't open his eyes when someone leaned in close to his face. He smelled breathy eucalyptus and cheap cologne. He held his eyes closed tight. A pair of lips leaned gently onto his ear, close enough to raise the hair on his arms and on the back of his neck. "Fucking nigger," they said gently, as if to a child. Brutus didn't recognize the voice. The footsteps receded again at a casual pace, and the door closed. Sparky stirred in his bed, maybe laughed.

Now Brutus could get a little sleep. He drifted in and out of consciousness, waiting a full hour after the footsteps disappeared down the hall. Before the first morning light could invade the room, he stood and pulled on a pair of jeans and a heavy gray sweatshirt from which he had decided against removing the stitched-on TEMPLE. It wasn't a corporate logo, not in the usual sense. A strip of duct tape on the outside of the bag had a note written on it: EVE & ADAMS KATONA J. U. I BP.

BP meant Budapest. A courier job up to the city. He considered his options, but the reality of the situation was that he had no choice. No say in the matter whatsoever. His own government was blackmailing him, and there wasn't a goddamned thing he could do except go along with it and try to keep his ass in one piece.

Brutus removed the tape, committed the address to memory, and placed it in yet another envelope to his sister. He dropped the envelope into the duffel bag along with his spare clothes, but resisted the desire to look inside. He also threw in his walkman and a vinyl booklet of CDs. From the weight, the bag contained either weapons or gold bars—and there was no way Sullivan would send a brother out into the world with a sack full of gold. But Brutus didn't want to know for sure until he was gone. Didn't want an excuse to back out—not that that was an option. He could still smell the aftertaste of the soldier's cough drop. The feeling of the man's lips on his ear reminded him of Magda's heavy breathing. He regretted not grabbing the cocksucker by the throat when he had the chance and gouging the man's eyes out with his thumbs, like they had taught him in basic training.

He stopped on his way out. "Take it easy, Sparky," he said, and stole his roommate's sidearm, replacing it with his own broken one. Sparky didn't stir, but Brutus knew that he had heard him. Punk.

It was cold as fuck outside. A small private jet taxied on the runway inside the barbed-wire perimeter of the restricted zone. Brutus didn't want to risk stealing a truck. The guards on duty didn't stir from Heaven's Gate, their tiny patrol bunker. A wisp of smoke trickled from a metal pipe sticking out of the roof. He hoofed it toward the train tracks just south of the base. He could get there before the sun came up, catch a train up to Budapest. Drop the bag. Get on another train. Back in no time. He just might live long enough to poke Magda some more. Getting off the base didn't worry him as much as how he would get back in later.

He used the handles of the duffel bag as shoulder straps and wore it like a backpack. The contents shifted and jammed something hard into his spine but he didn't stop to rearrange it. The cold rarely bothered him this bad.

There seemed to be no one else out on the streets except a couple of mangy-looking stray dogs, which he avoided. He stayed off the roads anyway and kept as far as possible from what looked like the downtown area of a small village. He put on his headphones to listen to the Roots. All the houses had metal fences around them. The Hungarians were a territorial people, no doubt because the Magyar tribes had been attacked and exiled from every homeland they ever had, until they finally settled there. Most of the yards had tiny vineyards of just two or three rows of vines and fruit trees that were now bare for the winter. Ice stuck to the branches like that chalky Christmas snow in Wanamaker's windows. Black Thought sang in Brutus's ears:

A revolution's what it's smelling like, it ain't gonna be televised
Governments is hellified, taking cake and selling pie
I ain't got a crust or crumb, to get some I'd be well obliged
Murder is commodified, felon for the second time
Never was I into chasing trouble, I was followed by it
Facing trouble with no alibi, had to swallow pride
Vilified, victimized, penalized, criticized
Ran into some people that's surprised I was still alive

He headed south, crossing over an empty highway and continuing along an endless dirt road. He couldn't see a goddamn thing, but he had heard trains down there somewhere so he kept going. Despite the circumstances, it was a joy to be off the base. Brutus walked for an hour before he found the tracks, which he blindly followed east until reaching a tiny backwoods train station—a concrete shack of one open-air room, now yellowed with old paint and cigarette smoke. He might as well have been in Chehaw. The graffiti was extensive and poorly done. A long wooden bench lined the perimeter, interrupted only by the gated and padlocked ticket window and doors to the men's and women's rooms, which were denoted by metal cartoon cutouts of children peeing. Swinging double doors led to the platform out back. The place was completely deserted except for a solitary sleeping bum. He looked frozen to death.

The posted schedules looked nothing like SEPTA's back home, but from what Brutus could gather the trains to Budapest ran every couple of hours all night long. If he waited long enough, maybe he could catch one to Vienna or Warsaw or Zagreb instead. Border security would be tightest this close to the base, though. He didn't have any forints but assumed he could make do with hard currency until he found a bank. He kept an eye on the sleeping dude, not sure if he was really asleep after all. Sullivan would have spies everywhere. These people really *were* out to get him. Brutus sat at the end of the room, where he could see the doors both to the street and to the tracks. He resisted the urge to open up the bag. The station was unheated, and he waited for forty-five minutes before a train whistled in the distance. He hid near the platform as it pulled to a grinding halt. No one got off except a MÁV conductor in a blue uniform and red hat, who wobbled to the end of the five-car train and signaled up to the engineer with a flashlight. Brutus took off his headphones and emerged from the shadows of the station, startling him. "Budapest?" he asked.

"Ja, Budapesht," the old dude said, correcting Brutus's pronunciation. Hungarian civilians typically spoke some mishmash German to all foreigners, regardless of their actual nationality. His mustache drooped from the constant assault of breath that smelled like onions sautéed in kerosene.

"How much?" Brutus produced a few bills of smaller denominations. He handed the guy a twenty. "This good?" The conductor took it and wandered slowly back up to the hissing engine. Brutus climbed through the nearest door.

The train was empty except for a few old men chain-smoking unfiltered cigarettes. Despite the vast number of free seats, they stood at the windows, spitting into the empty night. The entire train smelled like piss, stale beer, and more piss. Brutus went into an empty compartment. Four sepia-toned photos depicting the history of Hungarian railway innovation decorated the walls. Someone had scratched a swastika into the plastic covering of one. Another had the white remains of a sticker over the front of a trolley. Brutus slid the glass door shut, secured the lock, and closed the curtains. Then he removed his belt and ran it through the armrest of his red bench seat and through the handles of the bag.

The train lurched and then rolled eastward. Eventually, it would turn north.

The bag contained six assault rifles—Hungarian-made AMD-65s—each wrapped in a thick, chamois bag. So it *was* weapons after all. Upon closer inspection, they turned out to be semiautomatics that someone had converted by hand to fully auto. Totally illegal back in the States and likely in Hungary too.

Now he got it: he was going to meet some scraggly motherfucker with a goofy accent and an eyepatch at a table in the back of some dark bar. Hand over the bag, drink a whiskey, and, depending on how things pan out, either head back to Taszár or get out of the country by any means possible.

In addition to the rifles and his clothes, the bag also contained a map of Budapest with a red circle around a street corner next to the Danube and an Arden edition of *Julius Caesar*. No passport. Brutus removed his jacket and sat down to think things over. There were a few different ways the day could play out. In one scenario, Sullivan would wait until Brutus arrived at Eve and Adam's and then wash his hands of him. In another, M.P.s would snatch his ass off the streets so no word of the operation got back to the base.

Brutus typically didn't mind the M.P.s too much. He could handle them just like he could, and had, any pigs back home—yessuh, nossuh, anything you say, suh—or he could pop one and watch the rest scatter. But he certainly didn't want to get tangled with any corrupt elements of the corps, not if it could be avoided. They were a mean bunch of motherfuckers. Sullivan's kind of people. That was what now worried him. Once Brutus delivered the bag, Sullivan would have to send the marines after him. The same dudes who had been down to Taszár. That visit had been part of Sullivan's plan all along. They had come to the base for the sole purpose of choosing their guinea pig. They needed someone expendable. Fuck. Brutus would never be allowed near the base again. He was too much of a liability. It would be that asshole sergeant and Doornail and those guys—whatever the fuck their stupid names were—hunting him down. No question. And without a passport, he was trapped.

His army career was officially over. Funny—that was exactly what he had wanted so badly the past few months, but not like this. Another of Sullivan's jokes. You want out of the army, boy, you can have out. The marines would pick him up at Eve and Adam's or on the train back to Taszár and that would be it. Throw him out the window like a cigarette butt.

Sullivan would betray him—maybe he already had—but Brutus couldn't skip the drop. Any tiny hope of salvation depended on the timely delivery of the weapons. Anything else would be sure suicide.

There was nothing to see out the window but his reflection. He unholstered Sparky's sidearm and saw at once that it wouldn't fire. Anticipating the theft, Sparky had switched their weapons before Brutus did, the cocksucker. Now he would be without a piece, except for the ones meant for delivery. It had been a little while since he had fucked around with an AMD.

The cabin felt insufferably hot. The heater under his seat charred the backs of his legs to a juicy, tender medium-well, and someone had bolted the window shut. He was sweating like crazy but didn't risk opening the door. No telling who else was on the train. He picked up *Julius Caesar* and flipped through it, the pages sticking to his fingers, until he found that someone had highlighted a passage in yellow:

There was a Brutus once that would have brooked
Th'eternal devil to keep his state in Rome
As easily as a king.

Fucking-a right. Brutus wouldn't tolerate a king any more than he would tolerate the devil himself. An empire or a republic—that was *still* the issue, the reason he was in Hungary at all. It had been two or three years since he had last read it, but the thing he liked the most about *Julius Caesar* was that there was no definite good guy or bad guy. Brutus and Caesar, they were both good and bad at the same time. The reader was supposed to think Brutus was evil after he wetted his friend, but he turned out to be the cooler of the two.

When he felt himself drifting off, Brutus locked his arms in a sleeper hold around the duffel bag. The *click-click clack click-click clack* of the train invaded his thoughts and sounded like a metalsmith banging at an anvil. He dreamed of a large gray rat getting nailed to a tree. Brutus couldn't see who was doing it, only a pair of gloved hands holding an iron railroad spike and a huge Soviet-looking mallet. Unlike the rat in that marine's story, though, this one was still alive. It kicked and writhed wildly on the nail, screeching in verminous agony.

7.

Budapest approached and Brutus was neither awake nor asleep until the stench of cigarette smoke and piss seeped back into his consciousness and clothes. Sweat soaked his T-shirt and shorts. *Julius Caesar* lay prostrate on his stomach; he had read about half, up to where the emperor bit it. Among his dreams he remembered one about fucking Madga and another in which he stabbed Sullivan repeatedly in the back, like in the play. One of them woke him up aroused. His mind whirred immediately to life, recharged and ready to get through the day without taking a marine-sponsored dirt nap in some cold Budapest alley.

Short of discovering a Hungarian Underground Railroad, there existed only one viable possibility. He could play along, at least at first. Buy himself a little more time. Once Sullivan declared him AWOL, if he hadn't already, there would be no way for Brutus to prove that he was set up and blackmailed. In the meantime, he could carve out some breathing space. He would make like Houdini, his childhood hero. As a kid, Brutus had read every book he could find about the escape artist, but only one of them got into specifics about how to get out of chains and locks and burlap bags. He had studied it zealously. From then on, every Christmas and family gathering included an appearance by the escape artist the Great Brutini. His uncles would seal him up in his Chewbacca sleeping bag, his head sticking out the top. They tied ropes around him, then dropped him on the living room rug. He escaped every challenge, even after they got smart and tied him up before he went in the bag. Brutus's trick—O.K., Houdini's—was to bulk his muscles up while they hog-tied him. Make himself bigger. When they were done making all the knots, he slackened his arms for a little extra wiggle room.

He decided to deliver the weapons. But first he was going to make himself bigger.

Brutus would be safe until he got to Eve and Adam's. The weapons were worth more to somebody than Brutus's life, so whoever was expecting them might not fuck with him unless he deviated from the plan. But he certainly wasn't going to take any chances by showing up in a strange city with his dick in his hand, just waiting to get picked up off the streets. It wasn't like there would be a man in a chauffeur uniform on the train station platform holding up a printed AWOL NIGGER sign waiting to escort him to the drop site.

He pictured how it would go down. After Brutus makes the delivery, someone at Eve and Adam's will jump on the phone, beep Sullivan, and give him the all-clear to send in the marines. Any way Brutus looked at it, he was fucked. That realization made him angrier than he had ever been in his life. Hatred burned the lining of his stomach. If he was going down, he would take Sullivan down with him. Brutus punched the seat across from him as hard as he could. Lefts and rights. Sweat poured off him, and he kept grunting and punching until the fabric burned his knuckles.

A steady trickle of wind entered through the rubber ring struggling to hold the window in place. The crystalline lattice of frost on the glass framed a view of nothing. He wiped the steam away with his elbow and brought his breathing back under control. The tiniest bit of light crept over the horizon. Cold, frozen ground. Dead, flat farmland occasionally interrupted by the odd silhouette of a house or a hunter's wooden roost.

Brutus stood. Stiffness seized his shoulders. He cracked his neck and pumped his arms like he was rowing a boat, then put on his jacket and looped the handles of the bag around his wrist. He unlocked the compartment door and it slid open. A wave of stale smoke burned his eyes. Pairs of old men stood at the open windows sharing plastic jugs of wine. They argued above the noise of the tracks, but paused long enough to watch Brutus emerge. Each one pulled his bags closer or squeezed them tighter between his knees. Brutus gave them his best don't-fuck-with-me glare, but the truth was that he would've much rather been out there trading lies with those guys than playing FedEx for Sullivan.

He found a closet-sized bathroom at the end of the car and took his time pissing, all the while holding the bag tight. He rinsed his hands with cold water and wiped them on his blue jeans. He couldn't wait to get off that fucking train. The old men got quiet again as he passed, like he could understand what they were saying anyway. Back in his compartment, he watched the countryside morph into towns spaced closer and closer together and then into factories and the sprawling red-brick complexes of urban life.

"Budapesht"—that was how Magda said it.

He looked forward to taking care of business and then, just maybe, touring a bit of the city. The pictures he had seen of the city were so complex he couldn't make sense of them. The Hungarians lived and worked in buildings constructed before Columbus first occupied America. They built commie high-rises on top of art-deco apartments on top of ornate Gothic churches. One conquering army after another. Stone Turkish baths on top of Roman colosseums on top of Celtic tribal sites dug into the ground where cavemen first discovered the hot springs seeping out of the Buda Hills. Of course all of it was now crowned by America's contribution to the history of architecture, the Golden Arches. His stomach grumbled—it was a guilty pleasure, but a cheeseburger, or four, would've been right on time. He wanted to see a Roman amphitheater. The lions imported to Hungary—then called Lower Pannonia—really did survive on a steady diet of Christian meat. That wasn't just bullshit.

He unfolded the map of the city. The train was going to drop him off on the Buda side of the river, at a place called Déli Pályaudvar, the southernmost of the city's three major train stations. From there, he would need to get across the Danube to Pest. Eve and Adam's was smack-dab in the middle of town, near Margit Bridge. It looked like a serious hike from the station.

Despite his efforts to relax and save his strength, every mile closer to Budapest got Brutus's mind working faster. With no way of telling what was coming next, he attempted to focus his attention on the task of keeping his ass in one piece. Those jarheads could be waiting for him as the train rolled in. The M.P.s or the marines wouldn't even need to be in on Sullivan's scheme. If they were to pick him up off the streets, it would come down to Brutus's word against his commanding officer's, and that debate would never favor a PFC. In coming up with a game plan, his erring on the side of caution might make the difference between freedom—or what passed for freedom—and doing time in the army's penile colony. Getting got. He would get off at the stop before Déli even though that was farther from where he needed to end up. The map said "Kelenföldi pu."

Or . . . he could drop the bag somewhere else in Budapest, leave word for Sullivan where the weapons were at, and split. By the time Sullivan found the cache, Brutus could be back on one of these disgusting trains down to Serbia, or someplace where they would never think to look for him. From there, he could blow the whistle or even just wait it out a year or two until the smoke cleared and they had forgotten all about him. Did going AWOL have a statute of limitations? If he bailed and they didn't catch him in, say, a year, shouldn't he be able to go free? Fuck, CNN was down in Yugoslavia all the time. He could give those propaganda-spewing fools the scoop of a lifetime, except that they were too liable to turn him in. He could enlist Magda's help or even have Joan beep that Congressional bitch who only showed up around the neighborhood every couple of years when she wanted votes. His sister would know what was up any day now, as soon as she got that letter. Getting over the border would be tough even if he had his passport, but given the general fucked-up nature of all things Yugoslavian, he felt confident he could manage it somehow. Nothing was ever easy. Walking around Serbia at night couldn't be any more dangerous than growing up in West Philly. At least there was no crack in Belgrade, or probably less crack anyway, and given the choice, Brutus would prefer to take his chances with protomilitary gang lords wielding automatic weapons than with twelve-year-old Crip wannabes any day. He could even keep one of the rifles he was supposed to deliver, or sell them himself on the open market.

The outskirts of the city looked asleep. Closely compacted neighborhood blocks fit together at strange angles. Cages of chicken- and barbed wire ensnared each personal fiefdom of slapped-together brick, stucco, and plywood. Smoke escaped from roofs and blended with the slowly brightening sky. Brutus counted the stations on the map. Kelenföldi was next. He had a basic plan. He would hide the weapons somewhere and get the word to Sullivan about where to find them. He took several deep breaths and passed the old men again as the train arrived at a painfully slow, lazy stop. There were no announcements. He stepped down onto the platform and got swallowed by the pale yellow fluorescence that shone on the strip of bare concrete they considered a train station. AWOL—that was the reality of the situation. He didn't even want to think about that shit.

8.

There wasn't a marine or even a cop in sight, just an old drunk sitting on a bench with his head hanging. When Brutus approached, the bum vomited a steamy shower of blood into his own cupped hands and onto the ground between his legs. He tried to say something to Brutus but retched repeatedly instead and choked on his own words. Bile ran in a thin stream to the edge of the sidewalk and down to the stones lining the track bed. Brutus hurried past, watching his step.

Welcome to Budapest.

An oppressive, all-encompassing frustration nearly disentangled Brutus's thoughts from his anger. Every effort to distance himself, for the time being, from the hatred inside brought a sticky, nauseating substance boiling up from his gut. Brutus had never seriously contemplated taking another man's life, but here, freezing his ass off in goddamn Budapest, and walking through some homeless motherfucker's puke, he knew that given the first opportunity, he would set Sullivan on fire and shit on his ashes. In the meantime, though, he needed to get it together. Walking around all pissed off would only get himself got.

A flight of steps led down from the platform. Advertisement posters—Ivory Soap, Pick salami, Symphonia cigarettes, Unicum—covered the walls of the underground passageway, but they were awash in colorful graffiti and more than a few swastikas. While it was true that right-wing parties were getting reelected all over Eastern Europe, Brutus never dared to suspect that genuine fascism would rise again. Enough of that shit appeared unnoticed by the masses in the rhetoric of even the more moderate political parties at home and abroad.

He emerged in a cramped and ugly suburban neighborhood. No cars on the road yet. The train rattled away without him toward the city. He half hoped that Sullivan *did* have those marines waiting for him down the tracks at the next station. Suckers.

The smell of burning wood followed him. It hadn't snowed yet—the storm that hit Taszár would likely follow a few hours behind him. On the corner, a street sign affixed to the side of a house read XI. THÁN KÁROLY UTCA. The map indicated that he could take the road he was on all the way across town to the Danube. His immediate priority was to get someplace where he might not attract as much attention as out here in the burbs. Eventually he arrived at a bigger street, where Budapest looked more like a city. While he obviously wasn't in the fashionable part of town, the wide avenue—easily twice as big as Broad Street—looked majestic compared to Philadelphia. The building fronts followed the haphazard curvature of the roads and formed a solid cliff face. An empty yellow trolley ran right down the middle of the road between the traffic lanes.

A few tiny cars puttered past with engines that sounded like souped-up lawnmowers and moved just as fast. When the sun hinted at breaking through the low tarp of clouds, the statuary and ironwork came alive. The buildings had red, ceramic-tiled roofs and strangely painted exteriors. Some looked like stone fortresses straight out of the Middle Ages. Red, white, and green Hungarian flags decorated every lamppost down the street. The ground floors contained shops and dingy bars and video-poker dens, all with ribbons of the same colors in their windows. Near the top of one building, two sculptures of men, each five times the size of a real man, held up the roof on their backs. Brutus stopped in a doorway to check the map one more time. The walk would take longer than he had anticipated, so he hailed the first passing taxi. It slowed, but the driver looked at him and kept going. Just like back home. He walked a few more blocks. Parked cars covered the sidewalks, and he had to dance his way around them until he could get a taxi to stop. He climbed into the back-seat, clutching the heavy bag in his lap. The driver was an older dude. A cigarette dangled from his mouth, and the smoke mingled with his breath and the car's heater, which was mercifully bumped up.

"You speak English?" Brutus asked.

The driver turned all the way around in his seat. "No," he said, with a smile.

Color brochures for strip clubs and massage parlors filled the seat pockets. Some kind of crazy violin music blared from the rattling speakers behind Brutus's head. It sounded like rusty springs squeaking inside an old, dirty bed.

"I need a place for this." He made motions like someone opening a locker and turning a key.

"Kulcsra?" The driver's thick mustache looked like the head of a dusty broom.

"Yeah, a Coltrane. Take me there."

The driver took the map and pointed to Déli Pályaudvar, the train station Brutus had just avoided. "Kulcsra," he said.

"No, no. I ain't going there. Where else?" The driver didn't understand. "Another Coltrane." Brutus made a circular motion with his finger around the map.

"Ah," the driver said. He held Brutus's wrist and used his finger to point at Nyugati, the western train station over in Pest. It was close to the big red circle, just a few blocks from Eve and Adam's. Perfect. Cigarette ash landed on Margit Island, the tree-covered oasis in the middle of the Danube.

"O.K., there's good."

"Akkor jó." The driver smiled.

Brutus had to laugh. "Yo!"

"Jó!"

In the speaker behind him, someone dropped a pregnant cat into a blender and hit frappé. The driver pealed off as fast as his little car could take them and started the meter, which reminded Brutus that he didn't have any Hungarian money. He pulled a twenty out of his wallet. "This good?"

The driver's eyes lit up. "Jó," he said.

"Yo!" Brutus said.

The yellow streetlights couldn't compete with the rising sun, which became a spotlight pointed at the whole city, and in it the old-world charm of the architecture gave way to a polluted modern metropolis. The filthy windows, cracked plaster, and bullet holes grew more apparent by the minute. Dirty mustard-colored paint must have been on sale when they built this part of town. The buildings looked ugly and gray, caked in car exhaust. There were tall buildings, but no skyscrapers. Nothing silver and shiny like in Philadelphia. But the details were incredible. The colors. People—artists—had spent real time making the buildings, but as the light increased, Budapest looked more and more like a city in an advanced state of decay. He tried to picture what Philly would look like in another two or three hundred years. He followed the taxi's trajectory on the map.

The streets popped to life all at once, and an avalanche of cars, people, and crowded trolleys appeared from nowhere. The traffic sat bumper-to-bumper like on the Schuylkill at rush hour. Budapest wasn't built for automobiles at all, much less for this many of them. After crawling for a few blocks, they got to one of the six or so bridges over the Danube.

Margit Bridge was four lanes wide, with another trolley line running right down the middle. The bridge was shaped like an elbow and halfway across, where the funny bone would be, a smaller road led down to Margit Island. To Brutus's right, a small observation balcony extended over the water. Tourists were already taking photos, and he regretted leaving his camera behind at the base. He'd probably never see it again even if he *did* get back to Taszár. Or he would scroll through the pictures to find a shot of his own toothbrush jammed up Sparky's ass. That was what the army was really about—the excuse to jam someone else's toothbrush up your ass under the pretext of playing a joke. He wanted to get back there to bitchslap Sparky just once. That wasn't much to ask.

Over on the Pest side, the parliament building came into view—spires and a dome and separate white marble wings that led in every direction. A man could get lost looking at a building like that. Structures so elaborate should never really exist outside a picture book, yet dozens of them lined the river; they were in motion, fluid, changing things. Many had huge neon signs on top. Several other bridges spanned the river to the south. More red, white, and green banners flapped on all of them. Behind him, back over in Buda, a huge statue of a woman up on an otherwise bald hill held up a huge leaf.

The cavern of buildings in Pest plunged him back into shadow, a man-made eclipse fashioned from century-old tenements; the first one on his left, overlooking a small rampart park, housed a McDonald's painted a yellow so bright that it shimmered despite the lack of sunlight. Brutus spun in his seat to take in the sights. The taxi passed already-busy pizza joints and supermarkets, the Budapest Suites Hotel, and all kinds of places he couldn't identify before the driver pulled over opposite a huge, glass-enclosed train station.

The Nyugati complex was incredible. Two cream-brick castles, one of them occupied by yet another McDonald's, sandwiched a hundred-foot wrought-iron-and-glass wall that housed the train station. It looked like a set out of one of those English mysteries that the Mambo always watched on PBS. He handed over the twenty and managed to get a pile of coins from the driver for a locker. The old dude used hand signals to direct Brutus to the far end of the station and down a flight of steps—he made descending Yellow Pages motions with his fingers—then handed him a red, white, and green ribbon with a safety pin through it. A miniature Hungarian flag. "Tessék," he said. The driver had one just like it on his collar.

"Thanks, bro."

Brutus held on to the duffel bag and stepped into the melee of rush-hour pedestrian and automotive traffic. Everyone wore paper hats and many blew little plastic horns and buttwhistles like it was New Year's. Kind of fucked up, but kind of cool. A citywide party. People were already getting drunk. A few of them stared at him. There still weren't a lot of black people in Budapest.

He waited with the crowd at the crosswalk, his breath suspended in front of his face. He needed to find a heavier coat. In the meantime, though, he struggled to pin the flag to his chest like everyone else, until a rave chick in headphones leaned over and with a smile helped him fasten it. The techno beat surrounding her was louder than the whine of the cars inching past. The light changed; she didn't look back, but it made him glad to know that the locals were cool enough. The day could work out just fine. A trolley, its windows thickened with fog, sat idly in the middle of the road waiting for the pedestrians to pass.

The station was far bigger than even Thirtieth Street, and the trains pulled right up to the sidewalk-level platforms. There were newspaper stands and florists and a crooked-looking money-changer kiosk along the side wall. The vendors had on hats and mittens and puffy, oversized jackets embroidered with the names of American sports teams he had never heard of. The Chicago Tigers? He needed some Hungarian money, but that could wait until he found a real bank. Human and mechanical activity rang through the station. The iron of the front wall held in place a curved glass ceiling that ran the length of the station, down to the far end where the trains went in and out. It was just as cold in there as outside. The smell of french-fry grease reminded him how hungry he was. He needed to grab a bite as soon as he stashed the fucking bag. People piled on and off a series of trains, and the loudspeakers repeated a bizarre jingle every few minutes. He couldn't understand the garbled, prerecorded announcements and suspected that the Hungarians couldn't either. A sign at the back of the station had a diagram of a locker. An arrow directed him to a set of broken escalators.

The smell downstairs, like on the train but worse, singed his sinuses. His boots stuck to the floor. The blue-gray lockers covered the back wall of a dim passageway that led back in the direction of the street. There were also beer stalls and a video-poker den, and a red sign pointing to a metro station and a big red MARX TÉR sign, a holdover from communist days. He looked around. No one had followed him or was paying any attention, so he placed a hundred-forint coin in a locker. It opened easily. He removed the map and some money from the bag then slid it in, closed the locker, and pulled out a key with an orange plastic knob. He tugged on the door a few times and found it secure. Then he placed coins in six other lockers, taking the keys. He put them in an inside pocket of his jacket, keeping the real one separate. He could send Sullivan on a treasure hunt if he wanted to. Each key would buy him a little more time.

Meanwhile, he was ready to pick up a bag of doughnuts and some coffee, then scout out Eve and Adam's. Given the hour, it might not be open, especially if it was a titty bar. If it *was* open, though, he wanted to pop in, get the lay of the land, walk out. One two three. After that he would get a better look at that view from the bridge, maybe scope out the island.

Brutus retraced his steps to the foot of the escalator, then felt a hard shove from behind. He lost his balance and landed on his stomach with a thud. One of the keys in his pocket dug into his ribs, breaking the skin. He tried to ID his assailants, but the toe of a muddy army boot hit his face at full force and everything grew dark. He heard his nose pop open like a bottle of champagne. Warm blood sprayed everywhere, and the pain seared through him as if from a cop's nightstick. More kicks came just as hard to his ribs and kidneys and legs. There must have been four or five of them going at him all at once. A white, celestial pain stabbed at his eyes and took over his entire head, blinding him. Before he felt his consciousness recede, it occurred to Brutus that Sullivan had been one step ahead of him all along.

9.

Somebody helped Brutus to his feet, which supported his weight better than could be expected. He must have been unconscious for a while. Everything hurt. Every goddamn thing. It hurt to breathe, to exist. Whoever did this to him was gone. At least one rib was broken, maybe more. The pain ran all the way around his side and up to his shoulder. A well-dressed old man with gray hair was asking questions Brutus couldn't understand. His head weighed five hundred pounds, every one of them painful. One eye was entirely blind.

"You are an American?" the old man asked.

It said so on Brutus's jacket. U.S. Army. He tried to respond but his motor coordination wouldn't kick-start.

"You were attacked by skinheads," the old man said. He sounded like a bad Dracula impression. His necktie was slashed in half, and it dangled over his chest in ribbons of colorful silk. "I will get for you a doctor."

"No doctor," Brutus told him. The less interaction with the authorities the better. He just wanted to catch his breath. "I need to go. Thanks for your help." There was blood all over his clothes. His CD player and watch were gone, but the money was still lined in his jacket. Maybe it had absorbed some of the blows like body armor. Most importantly, all the locker keys were still in his pocket.

Brutus left the old man standing in a small puddle of blood and who-knows-what-else. Instead of going back upstairs, he stayed underground for another moment, until his senses returned. He followed the dank passageway to the direction of the main ring road—the körút—ringing the train station where the taxi had dropped him off. There would be fewer people down there than up in the train station. It hurt like hell to walk, but apart from a cracked rib and a chipped tooth, nothing else felt broken. A welt over his eye made seeing extremely difficult. He had to find a bathroom somewhere and examine the extent of the damage. Goddamn skinheads? So it *wasn't* Sullivan's goons?

He came to a brightly lit underpass beneath the körút, where he had to wade through a crowd of old women, drunk revelers, and the free-range insane, all of whom were orbiting around an Asian hurdy-gurdy player who balanced on a one-legged stool and performed a rendition of what sounded like "Helter Skelter." Brutus looked for what little solace the collective anonymity of Budapest afforded a transient black man who had been visibly pounded to within an inch of his life. Escalators headed even deeper underground to another subway stop. A band of South Americans in brightly colored blankets played guitars and pan flutes and danced in a circle. Two cops followed a hairy, gangrenous homeless man wearing a Burger King crown. They looked at Brutus funny, but he ignored them and they left him alone. An N.W.A. song came to mind. The pain outweighed his need to eat something, but he still had to get some Hungarian money.

A TourInform office, which was a small, glass-enclosed shop squashed between a newsstand and the Non Stop Büfé, listed the international exchange rates on an electronic sign. He joined the line behind a series of American teenyboppers anxious to transmute their dollars into assorted tchotchkes to bring home for Mommy and Daddy. The smoke and stink of so many people caused Brutus to sneeze into his sleeve; the pain ripped through his lungs like a gunshot. The snot was camouflaged by the other stains. His mood soured even further when some asshole Utah choirboy in front of him turned all the way around and said, "God bless you." Brutus had heard about these kids. Mormons or Scientologists or some shit like that, godboys gathered like tsetse flies over the corpse of communism in the former Soviet states and now sallying around the metro stations or in front of McDonald's sporting their WHAT WOULD JESUS DO? badges and tabernacle haircuts—that shaved-in-back, moussed-on-top, Berlin-circa-1938 look. Sometimes they carried microphones. And of course they were American, every last motherfucking one of them. A few of them were even stationed at Taszár. The kid's front teeth jutted so far out of his slack-jawed face that Brutus could have opened a bottle of Dreher on them.

"Fuck you," Brutus said. He was in no mood and would have liked nothing more than to punch the asshole in the nose just to see what it would look like. "Maybe the devil should bless me instead. What do you think of that?"

"Ex-excuse me?" The other gangly rednecks in line turned around and recited their prayers while digging through their WWJD folders for the pertinent literature to hand out to devil worshippers. They used cheat sheets to find the appropriate Bible passages, but because they didn't have exact reading material for practicing Satanists, they struggled to improvise something while Brutus suppressed his desire to piledrive someone onto the dirty floor. Amid the commotion he pushed his way to the front of the line and handed over a stack of bills. The woman behind the counter thumbed them out one at a time while another of the kids made the mistake of tapping Brutus on the shoulder. "Can we talk? According to Romans 8:37—"

"Son, leave me the fuck alone."

The drone of the hurdy-gurdy sounded like five lapdogs fighting in a tin box. The moneychanger moved on to the first of her infrared anti-counterfeit scans and someone tapped Brutus on the shoulder again. He turned around this time and with both hands grabbed the nearest godboy by his starched white collar. He barreled him through the swinging glass doors and body-slammed him full force onto the ground of the underpass. Then he walked back up to the teller, ignored the fright in her eyes, and immediately collected his forints. Nobody said shit to him after that.

Hurting all over, but finally with some paper in his pocket, he needed to find a place to crash for the night. A well-cologned man brushed past him and whispered under his breath, "Change money?" but Brutus didn't acknowledge him. The hum of activity receded as he climbed a long ramp up to street level, as if the station's noise had existed for him alone and stopped entirely once he was gone.

The taxi had passed a hotel—that would be his first stop. The sidewalk squirmed with people, most of whom wore red-and-green paper hats. The ribbon the cabbie had given him was gone. It hit him: it was Independence Day, the anniversary of one of Hungary's aborted revolutions. The army traditionally didn't acknowledge the holidays of their so-called "host nations," much less celebrate them, but Magda had told him about it. No nation on Earth boasted as many Independence Days as Hungary, and today was one of them. The Ides of March.

He opened the map again. Eve and Adam's was about three long city blocks down the körút, right before the bridge. Even amid the mayhem of public celebration, he had zero chance of keeping out of sight. He was too conspicuous. People stared at him openly and without shame. His face had to be a mess and there was blood splattered all over his jacket. The cold felt good and kept him more clearheaded than he expected.

Upon closer inspection, Budapest wasn't all that different from Philly. The buildings were older and the cars smaller, but the shop windows looked pretty much the same. There were bookstores and pizza places with chicks in skintight skirts just like in Old City. Budapest was equally dirty, that was for sure. Graffiti everywhere, the car-exhaust stink, fast-food bags blowing around like crippled birds. The only real difference was that everyone was white. It was like being at the opera. And the weather disoriented him. If the sun still existed, it was hiding behind a canopy of pollution and the densest clouds Brutus had ever seen. It looked like it could start pissing down rain or snow or sleet any second. If you didn't like the weather, just wait five minutes. But that was true every place he'd ever been.

He stopped in front of a record store to check out his reflection in the window but couldn't make himself out. The lump on his forehead still welded his eye closed and touching it even gingerly sent a spark down his neck. He didn't want to deal with any Hungarian jibber-jabber, so instead of picking up some food at the little grocery store he continued to the hotel, where a monkey-suited bellhop stood out front trying to light a cigarette in the wind. He refused to even look at Brutus, who went inside to book a room and establish a base camp for the day's business.

The lobby smelled vaguely sweet, like a bakery, and the place was a whole lot more luxurious than the outside made it appear. A door on the other side of the lobby led to some kind of beauty parlor. The ugly bitch behind the desk looked at him like he had shit stuck between his front teeth.

"Can I get a room?"

She smiled and sneered simultaneously, and spoke with a vaguely British accent. "How many nights?"

"Just one . . . no, make it two."

"May I have your passport, please?"

"I don't have my passport. I was just robbed."

"I'm sorry. In that case it's quite impossible to—"

"Listen, lady. I'm an American soldier and I can pay in cash. Up front if you want. But I need a room."

He unfolded his new wad of Hungarian money and that shut her up. The bill came to over three hundred American a night. Maybe more. It was steep but fuck it. He was desperate. She was no doubt skimming a piece off the top for herself. That was the way it worked in this part of the world. He couldn't even blame her, really.

"Fill this out." She slid a sign-in form and pen across the counter. "Do you need some help with your bags?"

"I don't have any . . . any bags."

She placed an electronic key card in front of him. "You are in room 422. Enjoy your stay."

Enjoy *this*.

As good as it would've felt to go upstairs and throw some water on his face, maybe rest his eyes for a second, he decided against it. He was liable to sleep for fourteen hours. It was better to take care of business first. His stomach grumbled despite the pain; his next stop would be for some chow. And a change of clothes was in order. He had some extras in the duffel bag but he didn't want to go back for them just yet. He put the hotel key card in his inside pocket and went back out to the street. So many keys.

He had gotten sweaty in the lobby and this time the cold air outside bit right through him. He didn't like the idea of breaking out that "I'm an American" garbage, but with all the bullshit he had to put up with every day from his own fucking country he might as well reap some of the benefits once in a while. Fast food—that other thing he hated about America but sometimes there was no getting around it. He sure as fuck wasn't going to some Hungarian restaurant to have a Gypsy come to his table with a violin to badger him for money, and *then* get ripped off on the bill because he didn't know the language or the exchange rate. A block before the river, he got to the bright yellow McDonald's he had passed in the taxi. The manager came around from the back and watched Brutus while the girl took his order. She didn't speak English, but he got the message across. He asked for a cup of coffee and three cheeseburgers. When his food arrived, Brutus sat down to eat and every single person in the place watched him like he was an exotic specimen on display at the Please Hassle Museum. A middle-aged man walked by and didn't even attempt to conceal his fascination and Brutus finally lost it. "Fucking problem?" he yelled, spitting bits of cheeseburger at him. "This some fucking zoo?" The man averted his eyes and disappeared. A couple teenagers somewhere behind Brutus made jungle noises. The coffee was still hot enough to scald his tongue, but he gulped it down and went to the men's room to see what kind of shape he was in.

The damage wasn't as bad as he had thought. The real pain, he knew, would soak into his muscles and bones overnight. His mouth ached like a motherfucker and two teeth were definitely chipped. To his surprise, none were missing or even loose. He washed the dried blood off his mouth and from around his eyes, then took a long piss. The laughter and commotion stopped when he came out.

Back on the sidewalk, those fuckers inside watched him through the restaurant's windows. Following the map, he turned off the körút and crossed a small park, which was really just a block-sized patch of grass next to the river with a few drained fountains and some benches thrown around. The base of Margit Bridge loomed overhead. The sculptures in the middle of the fountains were wrapped in plastic and looked like some kind of modern art project. Kids sat around drinking wine straight from the bottle. They stopped to watch him pass. Someone was throwing up behind a row of plastic garbage cans.

The wind coming off the Danube sawed straight through his coat and sweatshirt, both of which remained wet with blood and sweat. Margit Island looked as green and peaceful as advertised. At the other end of the park, the black and yellow Guinness sign at Eve and Adam's beckoned him.

An immense wooden bar ran down the right-hand side of the narrow room, and across it a row of vinyl booths overlooked the river and island through a series of tall windows. A dartboard hanging in the back like a saintly icon was being desecrated by four thick-handed boozers who never missed the bull's-eye. Several well-dressed businessmen stood at the bar speaking a combination of English and Dutch. A gaggle of whores in fake fur coats accompanied them, smiling way too much and drinking unusually small glasses of beer. Someone had crossed the word TIPS off the wooden box next to the cash register and replaced it with SINN FÉIN. Brutus hadn't even known they were still in business. Some of the ladies looked at Brutus, but they knew better than to bother him. The bartender whispered something to one of the hookers, and she strolled past Brutus toward the door. He turned with a wince to watch her pass and found himself staring down the business end of her moneymaker. Instead of anything he might call pants, she had on a pair of shorts the same color, texture, and which served the same general function as the skin one pulls off the outside of bologna. They left the rest of her ass free to slap together like two flesh cymbals crashing along to the climax of Beethoven's *Ode to Joy*. The door closed behind her with a jingle.

Brutus sat at the bar and put his head down until the bartender ambled slowly over. He was a stout, red-mustachioed man whose age—

thirty? fifty?—could probably be determined by counting the red veins in his eyes.

"I'm afraid we don' allow sleepin' at the bar, not unless ye have a few drinks in ye first, heh. What can I bring ye?"

"Shot and a beer. Whiskey."

"Coming right up. Jameson?"

"Anything."

"Good man. My name's Jimmy. Lemme know if I can be of service. From the looks of things I'd say someone tidied you up pretty good, heh?"

"Nothing I can't handle."

"I don't doubt that. Lemme get ye those drinks, heh?"

Jimmy poured a Guinness and left the pint in front of Brutus to settle, then slipped through a door at the end of the bar. The ubiquitous remake of "Strange Fruit" came on the jukebox, reminding Brutus of the last time he had seen Magda. Was that just yesterday? Day before? It occurred to him that Jimmy might be his contact and, if so, he was likely on the horn with Sullivan right then. The Irish accent sounded phony. He reappeared and brought Brutus another beer. "Here y'are, on the house. Here's hoping yer luck'll change, heh?"

Brutus didn't respond. He buried his head in his sleeves again and only nodded off for a second but the resulting disorientation was staggering. The pain settled in and cozied up next to the humiliation of that public beating. The embarrassment hardened like scar tissue; it disrupted the clarity of thought he was going to need. The fresh pint and another double whiskey waited beside him on the bar as if the booze fairy had stopped by. He discovered some new contours while running his tongue over the ridge of his teeth. His neck cracked with an audible snap but all things being equal, he was in decent shape. If he had gained nothing else from basic training at least the army taught him not only to suppress pain but to work with it, to temper it inside him like a burning ember. The cracked ribs and the sore jaw reminded him that he was alive, that he was a U.S. soldier, however disenfranchised. He had work to do; he had to stay alive, get the devil off his trail. He drank the whiskey in one go and took a long pull from his beer. The cold liquid made his chipped teeth ache.

"Now what'd I tell ye about sleepin' here? At least let me freshen up that Jameson for ye?"

"Nah, I've got to run. What do I owe you?"

"Not a damn thing. These are on the house, Mr. Brutus."

All right, contact established.

"So, you're my man?"

"Yessir, I am indeed *your man*. And I couldn't help but notice that you're not carrying a parcel of mine. You wouldn't perchance have lost it, now would ye?"

"It's cool. I put it someplace safe."

"Well I might hope so." Jimmy leaned closer. "Just to be perfectly clear about this, you understand of course that you're not the first piece of shit army nigger Sullivan has sent my way, right?" He kept his voice low enough so the johns and hookers at the other end of the bar wouldn't hear. "And you also understand that any chance you have of ever getting back to your cozy bed at Taszár depends upon staying in my good graces?"

Brutus wanted to reach across the bar and slam that fucker's pasty-white face into the rim of his beer glass. He looked Jimmy in the eye. "Everything is safe. I just needed to scope out the deal here."

"The deal here is this: I will expect you back at five o'clock. Not one minute later. You hear me?"

Brutus looked at his watch but it was gone, stolen. "Yeah, the five o'clock whistle."

"And if for some reason you are not sitting right here at that time, I will personally see to it that the fires of hell are unleashed upon you, your family, and everyone who ever met you."

Brutus understood, at that moment, that he was going to kill this man, right before he took Sullivan down.

"Now thanks for stopping by. I got me a bar to run," Jimmy said. He smiled at someone over Brutus's shoulder. "What can I getcha, heh?"

"Korsó of Dreher."

"You don' wanna drink that Hungarian crap, do ye?" Brutus stood with considerable effort and made his way to the door. "Come again," Jimmy hollered at him. Potato-eating son of a bitch.

Five o'clock. Hopefully that gave Brutus enough time to lie down and figure out what to do. He needed a change of clothes, a quick power nap. A hot shower. He contemplated picking up the duffel bag first but would put that off until it got closer to five. Never knew who could be following him, and he wasn't exactly eager for a rematch with those skinheads. He had reached his quota of bullshit for one day and was prepared to fuck somebody up. But the not knowing—that was the worst part. He felt a little bit more buzzed than he should've been. Bad idea. Some hazy light now penetrated his bad eye, but his forehead was still sore to the touch.

It got dark early that time of year, and the park was now deserted. At the körút, a wicked wind came off the river; the rows of buildings focused it into a steady, powerful blast. He waited on the corner with the foot traffic, and when the light changed he crossed the street, over the trolley tracks. No one got near him; the other pedestrians maintained a buffer zone of revulsion or fear. He wanted to see the view from the bridge again but that would have to wait.

He stopped in a small shop with a Levi's sign in the window. Two wannabe hotties without one natural eyebrow between them stood perched atop four-inch heels behind the sales counter and gossiped back and forth, ignoring him. He couldn't make out a single goddamn word. A sign read "Farmers" above a wall of exorbitantly overpriced jeans. He grabbed a pair and a fresh black T-shirt, a three-pack of socks, and a pair of boxers with red cartoon devils fucking in different positions. They rang him up and threw everything into a shopping bag without as much as looking at him or shutting up for a single goddamn second. The bill was over 25,000 forints, which he calculated as something like two hundred bucks. He wasn't sure that was right.

More drunks crowded the sidewalk. They melted away from his path even as they continued to stare and occasionally jeer under their breath. More jungle noises found him. The tall buildings along the boulevard came in different colors—pale blue or mustard yellow or such dark gray that they blended into the weather. Most had huge windows but a thick layer of grime covered every inch. He could write his name in the pollution: Brutus was here. Spray-painted stick-figure squiggles and swastikas covered the posters advertising raves and *HVG* magazine. Brutus passed what looked like an off-track betting parlor and then crossed the mouth of a wide alley that led pedestrians into the gaping maw of the Non Stop Nirvana Night Club.

That same bitch was working the front desk of the hotel and that same sickly smell overpowered him again. He got into the elevator. A laminated poster advertised a coffee house on the second floor, which explained the odor. That last cup had burned the shit out of his mouth so he skipped getting another cup.

The window of his small room faced a construction site behind the hotel. The clock next to the bed told him he had plenty of time. He pissed out all the beer, then stood at the window again. Smoke streamed from all the rooftops. He cranked the heat up a few notches, undressed, and went to the mirror to inspect the damage one more time. His eye was opening up more and more, but it still looked terrible. The gash on his tongue grew worse because he kept scraping it on his busted teeth. His lips wouldn't stop bleeding. He turned the shower all the way to hot and stayed in front of the mirror until he could no longer see himself through the steam. A bunch of snot and blood dislodged itself painfully from his nose, and he crapped the McDonald's out of his system. The bathroom fan whirred. Fixing the temperature, he showered for what had to be half an hour, using a brittle, midget-sized bar of soap to scrub the piss and smoke and blood off his body and out of his hair. His strength returned, and so did his rage. That was one way the army brainwashed soldiers—by teaching them to turn physical pain into hatred.

He toweled off as best he could, set the alarm for an hour, and climbed into bed naked. No dreams interrupted him and he awoke feeling a little better. His body knew how to operate on little or no sleep, to store energy during short moments of repose. He ripped the tags off his new clothes and left the old soiled ones in a ball on the floor, except for his jacket, which was a mess, and the Temple sweatshirt, which now had a few stains that nobody would be able to ID as blood. Given the dropping temperature, he would need all the layers he could find, even if they still smelled terrible.

10.

He checked out his reflection in the mirrored walls of the elevator and found something wrong. Something was slightly off. His nose was still stuffed up and his lips continued to bleed from a combination of the beating and the dry air. Then the doors closed, blocking out the stale coffee smell, and he couldn't understand how he'd failed to recognize it till that moment. Magda's perfume. Someone in the hotel had on the same perfume Magda wore, which was impossible. But there was no mistaking it. He breathed it in and even with the pain in his chest, he allowed the scent to drift through his lungs and into his blood. The rush came as a revelation; it crawled into his muscles and relaxed his entire body. It was a sign. He felt renewed, ready. He would finish the ugly business then return to the base. Magda's connections at her company could help him deal with Sullivan.

When the elevator stopped, he booked through the lobby and out of the hotel. He felt good, or at least good enough to keep himself moving.

Even in the stink of that rotting city, he could still smell Magda in his nostrils. No mistake about it. Someone definitely had the same perfume on. He walked as quickly as his sore legs allowed through the congestion of Nyugati's underpass. The noise and commotion had grown even worse, but he saw no sign of the skinheads or even the Jesus freaks. A cloud of smoke hung from the filthy ceiling. Bums lined the walls of the rear hallway. They passed around plastic bottles of dubious vintages and tried to stay warm. Someone among them made monkey noises as Brutus passed. He pointed at a youngish guy smirking at him without teeth. "Just because you're homeless," Brutus said, his voice still strange because of the swelling in his tongue, "don't think I won't body slam your ass."

He stepped over the glimmering pool of his own blood, which now lapped at the torn remains of that old man's discarded necktie. Confident that no one was watching, Brutus opened the locker. The bag had grown heavier. He swiveled his neck as he passed again between the rows of homeless families, expecting a bottle, or worse, to come flying at his head. Their chatter stopped as they watched him go.

The fleet of tiny cars on the körút formed a four-lane parking lot that went all the way to the bridge and produced its own noxious weather system. Streetlamps and electric billboards washed the city with a sad damp glow. Everything still appeared fuzzy in Brutus's right eye, but it had become easier to discern shapes and movement around him. The cold air both revived and punished him in the same breath. The sky had grown dark, but there was still no sign of the snow he expected. With the Independence Day festivities winding down, a hostile depression colonized Budapest, occupying its buildings and subjugating its citizenry. Hungary maintained the highest suicide rate in the world, and now Brutus understood why. It got dark so early. Even the capital city was gray and listless; he didn't want to imagine what life was like in the small towns. Most of the people meandered down the street like zombies, though small packs of young people continued to make noise and smash empty beer bottles.

He stopped in front of the hotel to catch his breath and watched in shock as a bum lifted up a filthy child no older than J. J. so that he could fish his tiny hand into a red metal mailbox. They were stealing the stamps and throwing the torn envelopes to the ground.

Hopefully Magda had already mailed that letter home to Joan. Ten or twelve days. After he dropped the bag, Brutus would only need to stay out of sight for ten or twelve days, until his letter arrived and Joan got the word out about Sullivan's bullshit. No problem. Maybe he should have kept a copy of the letter for himself. What if Magda had forgotten to send it?

Or what if she had read it and turned it over to Sullivan? The thought had never occurred to him. What if that *was* her perfume in the hotel? It had to be. No one else had the same perfume. It was impossible, but she had been right there. Something was going seriously fucking wrong. It didn't make any sense at all. He breathed deeply, tried to compose himself. His mind was playing tricks on him again. He grew dizzy. He was close to breaking down.

He sweated profusely. The bag had grown so heavy that he could hardly hold it any longer. He had to get rid of it. He clutched it to his chest and ran, pushing past the other pedestrians on the sidewalk. People hollered at him in a language he couldn't understand. Still tied up in knots and chains and padlocks, Brutus got an idea, one that would definitely make himself bigger. A delay tactic that might buy him enough time to get gone. He stopped in the park and opened the lid of a plastic garbage can. The smell was atrocious. He pulled out a bag of trash and dropped the weapons in the can. It felt great to get the weight off his hands. He tore open the trash bag and dumped the fetid contents all over the firearms. That Irish motherfucker would love sifting through this mess of banana peels and broken glass, the half-decayed remains of a cat. He would tell Jimmy where to find the guns, then hop in a taxi and get out of town. Head for the Buda Hills, he'll say to the driver. Or, better yet, he could hide out in the forest down on Margit Island. Live off the land.

He stopped outside Eve and Adam's and tried to settle his heart rate. The windows were all fogged up. The beer sign shined down on him and the steam of his breath. People inside were singing along with the jukebox. He couldn't make out the song. Probably that "Strange Fruit" bullshit again. Fat tourists sang pop songs while trapped at the very heart of the abyss, only they didn't even know it.

Eve and Adam's was significantly more crowded this time. Some girl was tending bar instead of Jimmy, who was nowhere to be seen. Cool—that motherfucker was bad news. Brutus wasn't about to back down from a fight, but he didn't want to invite trouble from that dude either. The same stool was available. He planned to tell this girl where to find the rifles and then bail. Everyone was speaking English this time; he didn't hear a lick of Dutch, German, or even Hungarian. Without taking his order, the bartender brought over a pint of Guinness and a shot of Jameson. She didn't even look at him when he tried to get her attention. Instead, she walked the length of the bar, scooped up a couple thousand forints' worth of tips along the way, and stuck her head in the back room. Jimmy emerged to much fanfare. He waved off the drunken greetings from different gangs of regulars, who patted him on the back like he was some kind of celebrity. He took the stool next to Brutus.

"The fuck you think you're doing?"

Brutus struggled to keep his cool. He envisioned himself shattering a full pint glass over this guy's Lucky Charms–eating skull and then stabbing him slowly in the eye with the broken end. "Jimmy. Just having a little drink. You know. Buy you one? Hey, another beer down here for my man!"

Jimmy got up real close in Brutus's ear, like the motherfucker who called him a nigger while he pretended to be asleep. That was a lifetime ago. "I see that you're empty-handed. You have no idea what you're involved with, boy." Assorted drunks continued to vie for Jimmy's attention. "You are going to disappear, you hear me? This is bigger than you can imagine. Fuck with me on this and dental records are not going to help your next of kin identify your body. Because there won't be any goddamn body, heh."

Brutus tightened his hand around his beer, felt the smooth bulb of the glass on his fingertips. "You'll get your fucking weapons."

"You better hope so, sweet pea. Now I want you to get your filthy nigger ass out of my bar, get what belongs to me, and just maybe—*maybe*—I'll let you keep both of your hands, heh? If you're not here with my parcel in fifteen minutes I will place a call to some colleagues of our mutual acquaintance. After that time I can no longer guarantee your safety."

Brutus loosened his grip and took a long swallow. "They're very close. I just wanted to get the lay of the land here first." He sipped from the whiskey to buy himself a few seconds to think, then slowly put the glass back down. Pure fear coursed through his bloodstream. He could feel it in his fingertips, in the pulse of his neck.

"Good to see ye, Tommy!" Jimmy said to someone behind Brutus's back, then whispered again to him, "Do yourself a real big favor. Go get what belongs to me and bring it here, heh."

Brutus remained silent, his eyes fixed on the row of expensive booze behind the bar.

"And think of your dear Lieutenant Colonel Sullivan. Isn't he going to be disappointed when he hears you haven't been exactly cooperative?

But he doesn't have to know. We can still be friends, Brutus. Looky here—I have a train ticket for you to Kaposvár." Sure enough, he lifted the top of a ticket from his apron pocket. "Be a good boy and this day never happened, heh? Sullivan assures me he'll welcome you back, no questions asked. You have fifteen minutes and not one second longer. That little girlie friend of yours is going to be awfully disappointed when you show up dead. What's her name—Magda?"

"Fifteen minutes," Brutus said.

Jimmy smiled. "See, good. You're not the mouth-breathing retard I took you for." He returned to his regular speaking volume: "And now if you'll excuse me," he said, and merged into the welcoming crowd. "Ere comes trouble, heh!"

Brutus got outside in a hurry. Something didn't feel right. His legs sweated in his new pants. The normally centered part of himself melted into a swamp of bile in his gut. Every part of his body hurt again. The only way Jimmy could have known about Magda was if Sullivan had told him. And if Sullivan knew he had been seeing her, what did that mean? What had Magda told him? Now Brutus was getting all turned around inside. Fuck. It was so obvious. She wasn't going to send that letter because she worked for these people, for Sullivan and this piece of shit bartender. The past couple of months, this whole time, he wasn't trying to get into her pants—*she* was the one seducing *him*. Oh fuck. The whole plan was Magda's doing all along. From the very goddamn beginning. That perfume. Something deep inside Brutus started to slip off its axis. She had probably tailed him all day long, laughing behind his back, mocking him. It had been Magda all along. Magda attacked him beneath the train station, she and those CIA-contracted thugs from the camp's restricted zone. Not skinheads, no matter what that crazy old man said. Of course. Brutus must have been a nice little diversion for them, a brief respite from torturing Arabs.

The filthy homeless dude in the Burger King crown he had seen earlier was rooting through the garbage can next to the one with the weapons. Brutus panicked. He ran at the bum and shoved him to the ground. Two girls walking arm in arm through the park yelled at him. They spoke English, but he paid no attention. He pulled the duffel bag from the filth. The bum convulsed on the ground and for a moment, Brutus considered kicking him senseless.

For the first time in as long as he could remember, Brutus was in a position to decide his own fate. He could deliver the guns, or tell Jimmy where to find them, and it would all be over. But that wouldn't solve anything. It might save his own ass, but it wouldn't *solve* anything at all. What was to stop Sullivan from pulling the same bullshit again on somebody else? Maybe he and Magda picked a new sucker every month.

He felt sick. Feverish. He wanted to cry right there.

He took off in a trot, but not back to Eve and Adam's. Clutching the stinking bag, he reached the parade of traffic on the körút. He was being followed. He had been followed all day, chased by shadows he never even knew to look for. But even that didn't bother him now. There was one thing left for him to do and then he would be free. Free from the U.S. Army. Free from all the bullshit and hassle in his life. Free from Sullivan and the system that kept slavery alive and kicking. Something had to give. The bag had grown too heavy for one man to carry. He wove through the mess of bleating circus cars and over the trolley tracks. Car horns and angry hollering assaulted him from every direction. Brakes squealed. More car horns, and then even more still.

Lights dotted the Buda Hills at the other end of the bridge like a low-hanging constellation. The island was dark, free from the intrusion of civilization. That was where he was headed. His hands were filthy and bleeding from the broken glass in the trashcan. He smelled like garbage now, like someone's refuse.

The word sounded strange in his head: refuse.

The winter air couldn't dissuade him from his rising confusion and anger. It was so obvious now. They wiggled a bit of pussy in his face and he lost his shit. Fucking stupid. Magda was in on it the entire time.

No—that wasn't right. He *was* getting paranoid.

The wind on the bridge was astounding in its ferocity. The Hungarian flags flapped like they wanted to come loose and get carried away. The city lights of Budapest formed a spectacle downriver, a grid on which the paths of innumerable occupying armies and their brutal histories could be roughly plotted. Brutus was finally ready to escape his complicity with the most recent imperial conquest, his complicity with the Man. That had been the problem all along. There was just no getting outside of his complicity or outside the very language the army used to keep him in his place. There was once a Brutus in Rome. Even resistance oiled the machine. That would sooner brook the devil than a king. Only refusal would make it stop.

Brutus stopped at the stone balcony hanging over the river halfway between Pest and Buda. Car lights lined the banks of the Danube in streaks of white and yellow. The bag he carried and the keys, the false ones, were the emblems of all that was evil in his life, of the doubt and resentment and anger. Magda's betrayal—that was what bothered him the most. Cast them into the water, and he would be free at last. Only without them would he be whole again. He was laughing out loud when he pulled the locker keys from his pocket and held them straight out in front of him in a fist. The metal and molded plastic cut at his skin. He let go, dropping them into the river. No light flickered off them; the water made no sound as it swallowed them. They simply vanished.

His body stopped functioning. There was only pain now. Check the date, he thought—I'm all expired. He leaned forward and the frozen, metal railing burned through his clothes and against his belly. Watching the twinkling lights of the skyline, a slow smile spread over his face. The cold felt good somehow. Glorious.

He hoisted the bag onto the railing with the very last of his strength. As long as he held onto it there was nothing anyone could do to him. Brutus had the government by the balls. He knew enough to get Sullivan locked away for the rest of his hateful life, but that was not going to help him. It was clear now—no authority existed that Brutus was willing to run to. And with that understanding came his deliverance. Refusal was the only solution. He wouldn't play along anymore. With both hands shaking, he held the bag out in front of him over the water. It was full of poison, full of black magic ready to seep out. He was ready finally to let go of all the pain he had collected, all the violence in his life, and to move on. He would keep moving. That was all anyone could do. Find an island and live off the land. Opening his hands, Brutus watched the bag plummet toward the river. It fell for a full minute, for four hundred years, for an eternity, before it broke the surface of the water. Then it was gone, all of it. He took a breath and tasted the blood rising to his lips. It tasted like the freedom that had been there all along, his whole life, unnoticed until that moment.

The Empty Chairs

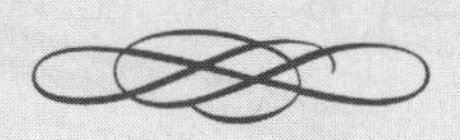

THE EMPTY CHAIRS

I.

Independence Day was three hours old and only Melanie and Nanette remained, the last customers of a bar with no last call. Even the prostitutes had gone home. "Bedtime, ladies," Jimmy said, pulling the plug on the jukebox and killing "Strange Fruit." He returned to wiping down the countertop.

Melanie still had more than half a vodka tonic left, which she swallowed in one long and breathless gulp. Nanette smashed out the end of another cigarette. They slid out of their booth and rose, unsteady, holding each other for balance. Jimmy leaned across the bar to kiss them goodnight. He smelled like a grease fire and had the gaunt look of someone nearing the end of a weeklong meth binge. "Sleep tight," he said. "See you tomorrow, heh."

"It *is* tomorrow," Melanie said. Her words sounded perfectly formed in her mind, yet she could feel her tongue slurring them. She needed to go home, get some sleep. She should've been in bed hours ago. She had a big day tomorrow. Which was today.

She and Nanette were American expatriates drunk on youth, overpriced Dutch vodka, and some sour substance they mistook for personal freedom. Eve and Adam's served as a second home, or perhaps third, a kind of base camp for their various recreations throughout the city. It was located on the ground floor of a bullet-hole-riddled apartment building next to the Danube, on the Pest side. Because the dimmed lights made it difficult to see from one end of the bar to the other ("Atmospheric!" one guidebook said, alongside a photo Nanette had taken) and offered a view of the Danube ("Scenic!"), Jimmy charged whatever he wanted for watered-down Guinness and packs of broken Chio Chips. He played up his campy luck-o'-the-Irish brogue when tourists arrived with stacks of newly changed forints. It was Monopoly money to them. As Budapest's only authentic Irish pub, Eve and Adam's ranked among the city's most tourist-infested and expensive bars, but it was definitely convenient. They lived just half a block down Katona József Street, up a mountain of stone stairs.

The cold air penetrated what few clothes Mel had on even before the lock clicked behind them and the round Guinness sign blinked off. Her hair, a thick, *Ride of the Valkyries*–blonde curtain, covered her whole back and was long enough to wear like a scarf, but even that couldn't keep her warm. The bar's exit was built into the corner of the block and faced southwest toward the southern tip of the island and the brightly lit Margit Bridge. The Buda Hills sat dark and dormant across the river. Living so close to the pub, neither of them had bothered to wear a jacket, though Nan did have a camera bag slung over her shoulder. Break-ins were a regular fact of life in Hungary, and the petty crime in Budapest was outrageous; she kept her most expensive and irreplaceable equipment with her at all times, and even there it wasn't always safe from the Gypsies on the metro. A few of her lenses, from Germany or maybe Scandinavia, were worth more than their respective cameras. Melanie should have been equally protective of her violin, which she bought in Austria from the same venerable firm that supplied instruments to the Vienna Philharmonic.

Instead of heading home, and to sleep, Nanette dragged Mel by the hand through the park at Jászai Mari Square and to the körút. There was no traffic at this time of night. They followed the tracks of the 4/6 tram, which during the day careened down the center of the four-lane road. At the middle of the bridge, a small observation deck hung over the water. Sometimes, when the weather was warmer, packs of drunken expats stood up there and revealed various parts of their anatomies or even peed on the tour boats passing below. A small pilot light of vodka in Melanie's belly emanated a pale glow that she felt all the way up in her face. They shivered and hugged each other for warmth, and Nanette tried without luck to light a cigarette. She got angry and threw her lighter into the dark of the river. Melanie had grown more or less accustomed to Nanette's outbursts. Their affection had recently grown somewhat less reciprocal than it once was.

A tanker passed lazily beneath them. The loud, mechanical drone precluded any chance of conversation. The ship was dark, though, making it appear like an apparition, an abandoned ghost schooner making its way slowly down to the Black Sea under its own steerage. The streetlights from the bridge fell onto the boat like candle wax. In an hour or so, the city would shut off all the lamps along the Danube, even at the parliament building and on the Chain Bridge. Mel attributed her fascination with the ship to the advanced state of her intoxication. She tried not to think about tomorrow's concert. Today's. When she focused too clearly on it, another warm wave of nausea tipped her off balance. She shivered again and held Nanette tighter. The vessel disappeared downriver, and in the absence of external noise she realized that most of the banging she heard had originated inside her own skull. This kind of intoxication, brought about by one vodka tonic after another, each intended to push her thoughts of the concert further away, carried with it a sickly, syrupy tinge. The queasiness was already starting to scratch its way up out of her stomach. She wouldn't necessarily be ill, but there was something crude about vodka's effects in comparison to, for example, the warmth of a nice burgundy or the gentle gravity of a Valium pilfered long ago from her mother's medicine cabinet. She stared down at the water.

There existed any number of mythologies concerning the Danube, many of which had floated downstream from Vienna—which, since the death of Webern, she felt safe to regard as the least musical of all the so-called "musical cities"—and were evidenced in such novelty hits as "Geschichten aus dem Wienerwald" and "An der schönen blauen Donau." One legend had it that the Danube only appeared blue to those who were in love. The river, called the Duna in Hungarian, defined and redefined Budapest every day, making it two distinct yet parallel cities divided by a shared mythos. Buda, on the right bank, was a land of large hills, grassy valleys, and vast stretches of dense forest. She and Nanette lived at the inner edge of Pest, the city's—the entire nation's—congested, urban core.

"Baby," Nanette said through chattering teeth, "I'm afraid that one of these nights the Creature from the Blue Danube is going to climb up here and drag you away."

"I hope it's tonight," Melanie said.

"Rrraawwrrr," Nanette growled, and broke free of Melanie's grip in order to swat at her with large amphibian hands. Melanie ran, hollering for dear life, chased in monster-like slow motion by Nan's extended arms and curling claws. She arrived panting at their building, but Nanette had the keys so she cowered at the doorway, waiting. When the creature finally approached, its mouth opening and closing like a fish's, Melanie put her hands to her frozen cheeks and let out a wide-eyed Hollywood-starlet scream. The sound reverberated down the street and bounced between the tall buildings. They cried with laughter as Nan fumbled with the lock. Melanie felt giddy and nauseous.

Their fin de siècle tenement filled the city block opposite Eve and Adam's. The proximity and height of the building across the street ensured their flat was in total and perpetual darkness even during the sunniest days of summer. A huge Coca-Cola advertisement perched atop their roof like a crown, visible all the way from the top of the hills. They could see the runoff light reflected in the other building's windows. When they threw parties, they simply told people to go to the Coke Building and look for their buzzer. Holes like the craters of Mars still pockmarked the façade where, in February 1945, it absorbed a significant quantity of German and Russian bullets while those two armies fought for control of the city. Nan finally unlocked the huge metal door and filled the entranceway with the same red light.

The elevator was broken again, or was still broken, so they hiked up the stairs to the third floor, which would have been the sixth floor in any other nation in the world, considering they needed to climb up six flights of stairs to get there. Their laughter and footsteps resounded through the inner courtyard, which was surrounded on all sides by landings that led to the apartments. Climbing the stairs never proved any easier drunk. Nanette had grown accustomed to dragging her camera bag to the top of everything from cathedral steeples to the rooftops of the prefab commie-condo high-rises of Békásmegyer, but each step required more and more effort of Melanie. She envied Nanette's athletic frame, but not enough to accompany her to the gym every night or for the occasional run around the island. Practicing her violin sometimes six hours a day, plus full rehearsals with the opera orchestra a few afternoons each week, took up way too much of her time for that. Every spring she swore to lose fifteen pounds, but obsession with her artistic growth, or her perceived lack of artistic growth, had so far prevented her from flattening her stomach. She felt distinctly fat all the time, especially in comparison to her sexy roommate.

Nanette possessed a rare, elemental beauty, the kind that made both men and women do surprisingly stupid things for her attention. Consciously or not, she flirted with almost everyone she met. Melanie saw it happen dozens and dozens of times at Eve and Adam's and all over the city. But Nanette was also violently possessive of Melanie. She had made threats in the past about hurting herself if Mel were to move out.

The scent of stale smoke greeted them in the kitchen, where dishes and glassware, empty wine bottles, and countless photographs covered every flat surface. Melanie's faces looked up at her in disappointment from the clutter. A doorway led to a short hallway and their bedroom, guest room, a spacious living room, bathroom, and water closet. Sometimes Melanie felt uneasy about being sandwiched in the middle of a monolithic apartment building, surrounded on all sides by a thousand people and their pets, but at least their building had the advantage of offering many other targets to any would-be burglar. All the same, they had added an extra bar-lock to the door to protect her violin, jewelry, and her massive CD collection.

Constant exposure to classical music constituted a big part of Melanie's job, of her art, and the fact that Nanette didn't fully appreciate that was a big reason why they had been fighting so much lately. The current, unsteady truce stipulated that Nan only listened to hip-hop when Melanie wasn't home. Nanette lacked the sophistication to appreciate the European art music—née "classical"—tradition, though she knew better than to complain about the extraordinary renditions of Bach recorded by the likes of Gertler and Heifetz and Serly. Melanie had long since given up trying to get Nan to appreciate serious music.

Something about the polluted fishbowl of expatriate life helped Melanie form lifelong friendships with people like Nanette, whom she very likely would never have associated with back in Boston. She still loved Nanette in a way, sure, but she also understood that her love was a matter of attraction among opposites. It was a love based on dissonance rather than harmony, with little more than passing, polite interest in each others' artistic careers. Melanie hadn't even bothered to invite her to the big Independence Day concert. No point, really.

In just a matter of hours, she would perform in the world premiere of an opera titled *The Golden Lotus,* by the world-renowned but way-overrated composer Lajos Harkályi. It would be broadcast live on national television and recorded for commercial distribution. If it turned out anything like Harkályi's other albums, it was guaranteed to sell millions. Not that *she* would see any of that money.

Nanette rinsed out two korsós, stolen from one bar or another, and poured both of them glasses of flat mineral water and totally unnecessary Unicum nightcaps from the freezer. They ate stale pogácsas; in the morning it would be Melanie's turn to run out for fresh bread.

There was nothing on TV at that time of night except soft-core porn, so she put on a Bartók album instead and forwarded it to the burlesque *Kicsit ázottan*. It was a private joke.

Nanette came in and promptly fell asleep on the couch without brushing her teeth. Her cellphone rang from the bedroom; at this hour it was either a jilted former lover or an editor asking her to go shoot a crime scene. Melanie didn't wake her. Instead, she finished her Unicum and then drank Nanette's too. When the Bartók ended she listened to Kodály's *Székely fonó* until she started to pass out as well. Rather than rousing Nan and dragging her to bed, Melanie let her stay where she was. She neglected to kiss her good-night.

Tomorrow was a big day. It was already tomorrow.

2.

Melanie lingered over a slice of thickly buttered toast and too-weak Meinl coffee until Nanette finally emerged, fully formed for the day, from the bathroom. Her third cigarette of the morning hung from the corner of her pouty lips. Hartmann's *Concerto funèbre* trickled from the living room stereo, barely audible in deference to Melanie's headache. "I'm getting my hair cut," she announced, fully aware that Nanette wouldn't believe her.

And she didn't. In Nanette's defense, however, Melanie had made many similar threats in the past. For months she had been talking about getting it lopped off, but always backed out at the last minute. This time she really meant it, though. Apart from the occasional decapitation of split ends, which she did herself, she had not had a real haircut since tenth grade, though recently she fantasized about stringing a violin bow with it. She wanted a new look. Plus, it was a complete hassle—an hour to untangle and dry it every day.

Nanette stuck her head into the kitchen and gave Melanie that glare of hers, an aggressive combination of disbelief and unwillingness to brook any dissent whatsoever. She was like that sometimes.

The night they met, the previous summer, a fight had broken out during a birthday party held on a boat docked on the Buda side of Margit Island. Melanie had noticed Nanette around town at Eve and Adam's and the usual expat hangouts—it was difficult not to—but they had never spoken. At that party, they found themselves at the same table, right next to the dance floor, and they hit it off over innumerable korsós of free beer. Nanette spent most of the evening dancing with an American soldier. A small group of them, on landlocked shore leave, showed up quite uninvited. They grew rowdier as the night progressed, shouting and slam dancing and trying to feel girls up while dancing with them. Nanette played along. She rubbed herself against one of them; they slow danced together for hours to the endless techno beat, and she returned to the table every so often to take a big drink from the beer glass that, unbeknownst to her, Melanie kept refilling from the keg. At some point, late in the evening, Nanette slumped into the chair next to Melanie and picked up a plastic instant camera that had been abandoned on the table. "I fucking hate these things," she said. "It's not yours is it?"

"Mine? No."

"Good. Smile!" She pointed it at Melanie and pressed the shutter. Then she held it out away from herself and took a crooked self-portrait. "Let me get one of me and you," she said and sat on Melanie's lap for another shot. "See that guy over there?" she slurred, pointing at a bow-tied Hungarian waiter who was being hassled and pushed around by the soldiers. "I'm gonna go take a picture of his cock. I'll be right back."

Nanette staggered across the dance floor, pushed her way into the circle of soldiers, and took the waiter by the arm. They watched in amazement as she led him compliantly into the women's room. Five minutes later, they emerged again and Nanette waved the camera at Melanie to show her that she'd gotten the photo she wanted. Nanette *always* got the photo she wanted, so Melanie learned that night. Frequently at someone else's expense. She sauntered back to the soldier she had been flirting with all night and kissed him on the mouth. He recoiled from Nan's face and then shoved her violently to the ground. The waiter tried to help her up, but the soldier smashed a half-empty beer glass against the side of his head. Someone screamed. Nan sat on the floor laughing and laughing, with the waiter crumbled next to her. An expat friend of Nan's took a swing at the soldier, which set off a free-for-all. Bottles flew through the air, tables got overturned, chairs splintered. Techno pulsated around the combatants. Someone dragged the unconscious waiter by his legs to Melanie's table, leaving a thin trail of blood across the dance floor. She watched in fascination, then grabbed her purse and joined the stampede up the gangplank into the summer night while the fight raged on.

Melanie sat on the curb outside to regroup. A cab pulled to a stop and Nanette stuck her head out the window. "Jump in!" she said, and Melanie did. "Well, that was fun, but I am *parched*. Let's go get a drink." She clutched the stolen plastic camera to her chest like a trophy. "I can't wait to get these developed."

The next day, when the photos came back, the last one on the roll showed the korsó at the moment of impact, before the waiter could react. Nanette had it enlarged, as she did the photo she took that night—the very first photo she ever took—of Melanie. The first ten pictures on the roll were of the birthday girl, whom neither of them knew very well, blowing out her candles before the party started.

It wasn't until months later, after Melanie moved in, at first to Nanette's spare bedroom, that she learned what had started the brawl. Just for laughs, Nanette had gone into the bathroom to take a photo of the waiter's penis, but once in the stall she decided to blow him. When she got back to the dance floor, she kissed the American soldier who, she said, had been harassing her all evening, and slowly spit the waiter's semen into his mouth.

That was Nan: willing to fellate a stranger just to get revenge for a perceived slight, no matter the consequences. Melanie adored her recklessness, at least at first.

"I mean it this time," she said. "Do you know a good stylist or not?"

"One that'd be open today?" Nan asked.

Melanie had already forgot about the holiday. She was also trying to forget about the concert. Her head hurt.

Nanette scrounged around for a clean cup and poured some coffee. Melanie had never seen her eat breakfast.

"You better think about it first," she said. She slurped her coffee. "I'd kill for hair like yours." Slurp. Nan cut and dyed her own hair, cropping it into short, stylishly uneven tufts. She sat at the table and flipped through the stack of envelopes, each one containing several rolls' worth of negatives. Slurp. She removed a few strips and absently cut through them with a pair of fancy medical shears. Much of her more artistic work—as opposed to the journalistic stuff she did for the local magazines—incorporated double exposures she created by cutting negatives apart and stacking them on top of each other while soaking them with light in the darkroom. She sipped her coffee some more and freed miniature portraits of Melanie from their backgrounds. She took a lot of pictures of Melanie. Too many, maybe.

"I *have* thought about it," Melanie said. "I need a new look."

"You'll regret it, that's all." Snip snip snip.

Melanie would deal with that remorse if and when it came, but right then she hated everything, *everything,* about her appearance and needed a change, especially because she was going to be on MTV—Magyar Televízió—in just a few hours.

In addition to teaching the occasional private lesson here at home, Melanie had regular work far in the back of the string section of the Budapest Opera Orchestra. Of Hungary's many full-sized symphony orchestras, the opera was the oldest, though no longer the most respected. Its prime passed long before Melanie arrived in Hungary. Over the past two years, she watched the budget shrink and with it the players' enthusiasm, including her own. Three solid weeks of *Tosca* to a near-empty house will take its toll on even the most dedicated musicians. And another prominent conductor in the city, a man whose artistic work she admired to no end, routinely raided all the best players in town for his own, better ensemble. She was one of only a few foreigners on the official payroll, and the only American. Her conductor found or invented every possible excuse for promoting less-talented musicians simply because they were Hungarian. But if nothing else, the job provided a paycheck, and no amount of practice time at home could simulate the sensation of surrounding oneself on all sides by usually competent musicians working toward a common end. And there was the occasional, sublime concert experience. On a great night it felt like sitting inside the belly of a fire-breathing beast.

For all the talk about fairness and blind auditions, she had no doubt that the best chairs in the Budapest Opera Orchestra went to the Hungarian musicians who happened to look great on stage. The same principle applied to every orchestra in Central Europe. There was no such thing as an ugly or fat concertmaster. That, sadly, was the nature of the music business. The entire system oozed with sexism and moral degradation. Sitting down in the pit of the opera house, she was hidden from the audience anyway. It normally wouldn't matter if she cut off her hair or dyed it as blue as the typical audience member's, but this concert was being held in a church over in Buda. There would be no pit, no hole to hide in. She would be up on stage and on live TV. She had to look good. She had to throw up.

Her cell phone beeped, signaling the top of the hour. The concert was at three, which meant she needed to be at Batthyány Square by two. Hour at the salon. That was ten thirty, eleven. Hour to warm up, play some scales. Change. Find a taxi. Two o'clock. Timing wouldn't be an issue. She *will* get her cut this time too.

"Whatever. But if you're serious, which I doubt, I want some 'before' shots first."

Melanie had a digital camera, which she kept hidden in the guestroom closet in a shoebox that also contained several Milka candy bars. She wanted to excavate it and get some snapshots to e-mail home to Mom and Dad, but she knew that Nanette would only give her grief about it. Her roommate never articulated the specific religious doctrine that opposed the operation of a digital camera, but it had something to do with the fact that it didn't use real light. Or the prints didn't. Something like that.

After dumping the dregs of her coffee into the sink—it was *still* Nanette's turn to do the dishes—Melanie helped set up a portable portrait studio in the living room. The only natural light in the place seeped through a set of double doors that led to a small balcony facing the top floor of the building across the street. By leaning over the rail, they could see a small patch of the river and island to the left, and of course the beer sign at Eve and Adam's. Even with the windows closed, a cold draft forced its way into the room. The sky, still a good month or two from showing any sign of blue, didn't provide enough light, so Nanette set up two softboxes containing all but one of the special bulbs she had found in Prague at the end of a long day spent dragging an increasingly grumpy Melanie to musty camera shops all over the city. One of them got broken, quite accidentally, during the train ride home.

Nanette went digging on her hands and knees in the hallway storage closet, cursing up a storm. She emerged with an antique wooden tripod and two white umbrellas. She placed five cameras of different manufacture and expense on the floor, then tested the room at great length with a pocket-sized light meter. She didn't say anything, but her body language complained bitterly about the endless Budapest winter. Nan came from California originally—*Southern* California, she always clarified, as if it were a different state—and talked about moving back almost as frequently as Melanie talked about getting her hair cut. Did Melanie give *her* grief about *that?* No.

A web developer whom Nanette used to sleep with, and maybe still did, credited the Soviet system for the Hungarians' reputation as gifted computer programmers and scientists. The government back then, this guy said, distributed very little funding to the scientific community in comparison to what it gave to the military, or even to the arts, yet it demanded results on par with the advances coming out of the United States and Japan. Those tech professionals who remained behind after the short-lived revolution of 1956 and their descendants learned to make do with substandard equipment and facilities and even to create comparable products despite the limitations. When the free markets opened up and new equipment came rolling over the Western border, the Hungarians found themselves able to use it more efficiently than their lazy, capital-fattened counterparts around the globe. That was the theory at least, and it was one Nanette co-opted for her photography. She figured that if she could make do with five months of miserable weather and poor light every year, by the time she got back to San Diego she would *understand* sunlight in a way somehow different from the local, art school–trained losers. And her approach was already beginning to pay off. The Ernst Galléria, one of the better small museums in the city, had included a series of her platinum prints in an international group show. The sequence, "Cinders I-XIV," titled in part after Cindy Sherman, included claustrophobic self-portraits of Nanette sitting on the toilet in a tight V-neck, with her nipples erect and panties at her ankles, pouring petrol on herself from a metal can, as if, most people thought, in preparation for setting herself on fire. A wet T-shirt contest done with gasoline. She never told the show's curator, but once confessed to Melanie that she really did intend to immolate herself that day. To record her own death. She never explained what stopped her, the box of matches already in hand.

Nan had some emotional issues. It got to be a bit much sometimes.

The critical reception of her "Cinders" earned her a job as staff photographer for a local English-language weekly, and her work also appeared with regularity in *HVG* and other national publications. She closed the curtains again in disgust. "You know what I want?" she asked.

Melissa had heard this a hundred times before. One great photograph.

"I want to take one great photograph. Just one, that's all. The kind of photo, like that Chinese student in front of the tanks at Tiananmen Square or the colonel shooting a Vietcong prisoner in the head. The kind of photograph that can take the symbolic—you know, something universal—and make it specific enough to tell a story about one particular moment in history. Make it iconic. Close your eyes."

The words didn't register quickly enough: Melanie was staring into one of the light boxes, humming along with the opera in her head and growing steadily more nervous, when Nanette switched it on. Melanie yelped.

"Oh, my bad. You O.K.?" Nan asked.

"No, I'm good," Melanie said.

Blindness took over, then panic, then the room emerged from a thick red gauze. Her headache swelled into allegro con brio and she considered going into the water closet—where she swore she could still smell gasoline—and make herself throw up just to be done with the hangover. Even as her eyes cleared, the white after-image of the light box.followed her view for several more minutes and projected itself onto everything she looked at, lending Nanette a ghostly appearance. For years afterwards, when Melanie would think of Nanette, she still pictured that glow around her.

Nan lifted a spinning saloon pianist's stool and sat Melanie in the center of the room.

Even with her trained and perfect string-section posture, Mel's hair fell past the wooden seat. Nan squeezed a few Polaroids first, which to Melanie weren't any better than digital pictures, and let them collect in the camera's mouth before they drooled onto the throw rug and formed puddles of changing color. Finishing the roll, Nan examined her compositions for a moment and, finding one or two that satisfied her, changed to the eight-by-ten. "I'll need all my color later," she said. "I hope black-and-white's O.K."

The bleak winter left bright windburns on Melanie's complexion, which was soft and milky otherwise, except of course for the permanent bruise her violin left under her jawbone. Standing over her shoulder, Nan said something about how the contrast between her cheeks and blonde hair would come out well with a polarizer, or maybe a yellow filter. She used the tripod for the first couple, taking the traditional hands-folded portraits, Mel's hair hanging over one shoulder. Then she shot from every possible angle: she snapped a photo, spun the stool a few degrees, snapped another, until Melanie traveled a full, woozy circle. She envisioned the freakish, pseudo-cubist collage of her own head that would result when Nanette assembled all the images, if she ever got around to it. The project required an entire roll, one Nan would need to develop carefully in the darkroom if she wanted every shot to match up right. Her sweaty, greasy-fingered editor at the newspaper would pay for the film and paper and developing fluids whether he knew it or not.

Nan unscrewed the camera from the tripod and started again with facials. She snapped them quickly, one by one, from every angle. "Hold on," she said, leaving Melanie sitting there, then came back with a flannel sheet from the bed. Next, she opened the curtains again and used the scissors to slice a manhole-sized opening in the sheet, which she then hung over the curtain rod to allow a different, localized shape of dull light to leak through into the room. She had Melanie turn her chin back and forth rapidly until her hair fluttered around her head like in a shampoo commercial. Until she grew nauseous. More nauseous. Last night's vodka had turned to battery acid in her stomach.

Nan made her sit perfectly still while she focused on minute details of her face. "You make a great subject," she said. "I'd like to get a couple shots of your back."

"Sure." Melanie spun slowly around.

"Without your shirt."

She didn't stop to think about it. It was by no means the first time she had posed nude for Nanette. She peeled off her turtleneck and twisted her arms behind her back to snap off her bra. "Pants too?"

"Not unless you want."

"I think I'll keep them on."

Nan plugged a fresh cartridge into the Polaroid and took more compositional studies before starting with an SLR equipped with a bulky automatic winder. She snapped the shutter, stepped back a few inches to incorporate more of Melanie in the viewfinder, listened for the whir of the winder, and squeezed again. She continued this until her back pressed against one of the CD cases. Melanie covered her breasts with two ropes of blonde hair. Nan tried to keep the mood jovial. "Life is so unfair," she said. "Why is it again that you got such big tits and I didn't get any?"

"It's just blubber," Melanie said, swearing to herself that this year, when it warmed up, would be the one in which when she finally got in shape.

Nanette reattached the eight-by-ten to the tripod and picked up another camera. "There's a couple color shots left in here." Losing herself in the gentle clicking of the shutter and the low, electric hum of the winder's toccata-like rhythm, she glided around the room, firing at Melanie again and again, stopping only once to re-check her light meter and reload with more black-and-white. Melanie contorted herself into every conceivable pose, giggling and spinning in obedience with her photographer's direction, trying to act natural. Whatever that meant. Their session continued for another twenty minutes before she grew cold in her fingers and nipples, even under the lights. She asked for permission to get dressed and pulled on her shirt again while Nanette put her stuff away. She never got around to using the Holga, which was by far the coolest camera in her roommate's vast arsenal.

"So where's this salon?" she asked, buttoning her shirt.

"Just up at the körút. What's that hotel right before Nyugati—the Hungotel?"

"With the good cukrászda? That's the Budapest Suites."

"Right. They have a salon. *Very* expensive."

"Not like I get my hair cut every day."

"True enough, baby. They're probably closed today, but if Judit's there you can just walk in. Tell her you're a friend of mine. I did some headshots for them that that fucking bitch still hasn't paid me for."

She will need to sneak over there right away. "What time you want to meet up later?"

"I have to shoot the prime minister today at the National Museum, or else you know I'd be at your concert."

Melanie couldn't remember inviting her. "You can catch it when it moves to the opera house," she said. "One of the singers in particular is amazing."

"And the conductor's supposed to be there?"

"The composer, yeah. Lajos Harkályi. I hope the conductor shows up too, though."

"Fuck you."

"I can meet you downstairs at five? Six?"

"Six sounds right. After the speeches there'll be parades and shit. I'll beep you if anything changes."

Melanie watched Nanette repack the rest of her equipment. Then they bundled up and left together, circling the landing to the top of the stairs. They didn't even bother to try the elevator. Stepping outside felt like walking into a city-sized meat locker. Smelled just as bad too.

"Looks like snow."

"It's too cold to snow," Nanette said, "but at least all the dog shit has frozen."

They walked up to the körút and took the tram one stop to Nyugati. The platform where they got off sat on an island in the middle of the four-lane road, between the glass-and-iron face of the station on one side and the shiny exterior of a huge communist-era department store on the other. A flight of stairs led to the underpass built beneath the körút and the train station. It reverberated with music and, already, drunken laughter and singing. Everyone wore red, white, and green ribbons. Their favorite of the many colorful local bums, the Fisher King, shuffled among the various street musicians collecting coins from passersby, his Burger King crown and filthy beard likewise decorated for the holiday. Nanette kissed Melanie good-bye and took the escalator farther down into the stinking bowels of the city, where she could jump on the blue line. Mel backtracked to the Budapest Suites. It was a relief to be on her own for a few hours. Away from Nan. The sidewalk seethed with revelers swinging plastic jugs of homemade wine and celebrating Hungary's almost-was independence.

3.

The Budapest Suites stood out even amid the endless series of gorgeous art nouveau buildings that lined the körút. Each possessed a unique charm and state of disrepair. Melanie's muscles grew tense as she approached the salon, which turned out to be open despite the holiday. Great news. Now fewer and fewer businesses closed for the national holidays; everything was open today.

A separate entrance for the salon steered people away from the lobby of the hotel, which appeared busy. From cold or worry, Melanie's hands shook as she pushed through the revolving door. She forgot, however briefly, about her burning stage fright. She wanted to remember to pick up some pastries from the good cukrászda upstairs on her way out.

The building's heat, cranked all the way up, enveloped her. Sweat licked coolly at the back of her neck and trickled down inside her shirt and cashmere sweater. An acute feeling of exposure lingered on her body from the photo session and she felt embarrassed, revealed in some way to the entire salon. The place buzzed with life and gossip and an annoying, standard-issue techno beat she believed undeserving of the term "music."

A half dozen people in the reception area smoked English cigarettes and dropped the ashes into their own and others' glasses of sparkling wine. Whatever excitement she felt about her pending new look faded in a spritz of fruit-scented hairspray. Everyone else looked like models, but she was chubby and gross. As an expat, she had grown accustomed to the locals' sneers and snide looks—not everyone appreciated the presence of such a large and affluent foreign population. In the eyes of those present, she was no doubt contributing to the stereotype of the ugly American. The disdain was palpable.

"Do you speak English?" she asked the woman behind the desk. The receptionist's low-cut T-shirt revealed enough of her huge breasts for

Melanie to admire the tanning-bed-induced, baked-potato texture of her skin.

"Yes," she said, exhaling loudly.

"Are you Judit?"

The receptionist's lipstick parted like a pouty vermilion sea. "Judit, uhn, is very busy. Do you have an appointment?"

"I'm a guest of the hotel," she lied, "and a friend of Nanette Oread."

The woman rolled her eyes and exhaled again. "Just wait. You can sit."

She stood and disappeared into the next room. As the frosted-glass door opened, Melanie saw a series of women having their hair washed by a band of white-robed attendants hovering over a row of sinks. The intricate motion of the various stylists, hair washers, and the occasional customer appeared choreographed, like a secret dance of the Hungarian nouveau riche. Women young and old prepared for holiday parties and gallery openings across the city. Some of them might be at her concert a little later. The nausea contemplated an encore. The most compelling people present were those with no apparent role in the unfolding drama, those who gathered only to watch and to be seen watching. She waited for what had to be fifteen full minutes before the receptionist came back. "Judit can help you today, but you must wait."

"How long?"

"I don't know—thirty minutes. Maybe more." She looked like she was made out of crinkly brown construction paper.

"Fine," Melanie told her, unwilling to be frightened off. She sat and tried to make herself comfortable.

Her Hungarian wasn't perfect, far from it, but it wasn't bad for someone who had never taken lessons. She understood just enough to follow the conversations around her. The ladies-in-waiting were agog over some Hollywood actor's visit to Budapest to shoot a film, and about a famous transvestite's appearance in that very salon just yesterday. One woman, accompanied by her daughter and her daughter's Puli, looked like the recipient of at least one face-lift that didn't take.

A glamorous woman of indeterminate age approached and said, "Kávé vagy pezsgő?" and upon receiving an answer fetched a hot mug of surprisingly good coffee. Vienna's famous coffee houses were just three hours away, yet it was still next to impossible to find a decent cup in Budapest. A little hair of the dog would have done her some good, but Melanie *never* drank alcohol before a concert. She sipped slowly and self-consciously, holding the saucer in her lap the way her mother had taught her. The usual magazines stood in perfumed stacks on the table, along with several unread, erect-postured hardcover books and current issues of the three local newspapers written in English. She flipped through one while listening in on the conversations around her. The caption "Nanette Oread" appeared beneath every photo. The cover story detailed the different Independence Day festivities throughout the city, and she was surprised to find a long feature on Lajos Harkályi on the front page of the Arts section. Much of it was lifted almost verbatim from the *Grove Dictionary of Music and Musicians,* but it was also more or less common knowledge. Born in Hungary, Harkályi had been sent to a concentration camp as a child, which was where he started to compose music. After the war, with the personal help of Eugene Ormandy, he ended up at the Curtis Institute, where he devoted himself to composing music full-time. He labored for years in obscurity until a small indie label agreed to release his Symphony No. 4 ("Musik Macht Frei"), which according to the Pulitzer Prize announcement, "fulfilled all of the obligations of the masterpiece while simultaneously looking back in terror and forward with hope of redemption." The album had sold four million copies and his subsequent recordings did nearly as well. Whatever. Sure, his story was tragic, but no one talked about the actual *music*.

A different woman finally escorted Melanie to the hair-washing area, where she was draped in an elegant silk smock and silently directed to a chair that tilted comfortably backwards to a sink of blue glass. She wished she had removed her sweater. Having her hair washed took forever because the woman used what had to be five or six different shampoos, conditioners, and rinses. She was leaned forward again, her hair patted down with a towel, then led to another room deeper in the heart of the hotel and into a plush, overstuffed version of a traditional barber's chair. Four of them lined the full-length mirrored wall like obese ballerinas. From where she sat, the mirrors in front and behind revealed hundreds of her own bright-red faces staring back at her. In the spotless silver screens, the flat motion of the salon behind her took on the elegance of a vintage black-and-white film, but her own reflections looked like they had been crudely colorized for cable TV.

A heavily accessorized woman, presumably Judit, approached. She looked angry. Before she said a word, Melanie panicked. She wanted to scream, to throw a blow-dryer through the nearest mirror. She could already see her reflections shattering. They tinkled and sparkled on the marble floor. She saw her severed hair among the broken glass, like some kind of lost limb that still tickled her scalp. She gagged. There was no way she could allow this woman to cut off her hair. She heard fabric tear as she pulled off the smock. She dropped a five-thousand forint bill on the counter, grabbed her coat, and bolted for the door. Everyone watched her in bemused disbelief. Melanie hated every last one of them.

Tears rolled down her face and ice formed in her hair. Unwilling to face the crowds back at Nyugati, and risk running into someone she knew, she pulled her coat close around her neck and rushed home. Four long blocks. She cried the entire way, uncontrollably, without any specific reason she could pinpoint. Nanette will never let her hear the end of it—she could be a total bitch like that sometimes. She half-jogged the entire way, sobbing into her scarf. Her teeth chattered. Clothes stuck to her damp skin. It felt like someone had dumped an ice bucket down her turtleneck. She couldn't feel her ears, and was going to get pneumonia, but at least her headache was gone. A pack of drunk boys in generic-looking blue jeans and bootleg NBA jackets came out of the McDonald's and jostled each other for her attention, taunting her with fake boo-hoo-hoo sobbing. She could still hear them as she slammed the apartment door behind her, shutting out the whole stupid city.

4.

Melanie stripped off her wet clothes and left them in a bunch on the kitchen floor. The whole room stank of garbage and sour milk and something so nasty she didn't even want to attempt to identify it. She shoved some pans off the stovetop and onto the counter, creating a chain reaction that sent an ashtray full of butts crashing into the sink. She ignored the new pile of broken glass and filled the kettle from the tap. She took a match from the box and turned on the gas.

Naked, the usual heat of the apartment felt about right. An ogre in blue overalls lived downstairs in the dank basement of the building, from which he controlled the heat with a huge lever mounted on the wall. Every November 1 he switched it from OFF to SWELTER, and every April 1 he moved it back again, regardless of petty details like the actual atmospheric conditions. What he did with the rest of his time remained a mystery. He obviously didn't work on the elevator. She and Nanette typically adjusted the heat by opening the living room windows and curtains to various apertures. None of that was necessary right then. Her ears and fingertips and toes still tingled. The radiators clanged and clanged around the clock; they needed to place bowls full of water and orange peels on them to prevent their skin from drying and cracking. The dry cold was murder. The kettle whistled, G-flat sliding up to D-sharp, before she removed it from the heat. Chamomile.

Melanie loved having the apartment to herself, even if it *was* a complete mess. Once the concert was over and done with she would scrub the floors, vacuum, dust. It'll be like therapy. She carried the pot, a clean mug, and an oversized Milka bar into the bathroom and set them on the floor, where they kicked up a tiny puff of baby powder. She avoided looking at herself in the mirror and then realized that she was avoiding herself, so she looked. Her face was puffy. Rings had formed under her eyes. She dislodged some remaining specks of ice from her hair. She was exhausted, miserable. So absolutely miserable.

The pre-concert jitters manifested themselves most clearly in her stomach, which lurched at the very thought of appearing in front of an audience. She wanted to throw up in the sink. Obsessing only made it worse. It was uncontrollable. She knew, deep down, that some day people would catch on to her—they would discover that she was a fraud and did not possess even the vaguest hint of musical talent. It was certain to happen. It could happen today. Today, she wouldn't even be able to hide down in the pit but, instead, would be up on stage in full view. On national television. The composer would be there. The entire nation of Hungary would be watching her. It would get made into a multiplatinum album.

The Polaroid and a few of Nanette's less essential cameras were scattered around the living room. Melanie ran her finger along a row of CD spines and it stopped at some piano music. The Diabelli Variations—Beethoven's simultaneous tributes to and parodies of his contemporaries. Anything to distract herself from the scene at the salon, from the impending opera. She didn't even want to *think* about her violin just yet. She hated that violin sometimes, just like she hated her job. The opera orchestra was just a stepping-stone until she could get up the energy to move back home. She planned to audition for the Boston Symphony one day soon. In the meantime, she slipped into the tub. The suds rose slowly to cover her belly. The music wasn't loud enough. Only the right hand was audible, the high end.

Slowly, oh so slowly, she felt her pre-concert nerves settling, as she knew they would. They always did. It was a terrible, exhilarating cycle: there existed a now-familiar transition, a fibrous layer separating her fear from the deep-rooted animal need to just get the concert underway. It was the waiting that killed her. Once it started, she would feel that gushing, can't-step-in-it-twice river of sonic clarity that existed nowhere else but on stage; that feeling was precisely why she had learned to play music in the first place, why she pushed herself so hard to practice. Then, at the merciful end of every concert, with the applause raining down, she would want nothing more than for the music to start anew, to wash over her one more time. She would want to run back to the top of the slide and speed down again, laughing, screaming. This first climb up was the worst part. Right now, with her fingers beginning to prune, she struggled to recall that sense of self-erasure, that lovely erosion of her ego in favor of an artistic experience she will share with the audience, the other players, even the conductor. The glory of cozying up next to the godhead for a few movements. She relaxed more. She had chewed through half of the candy bar. Embarrassed by her private gluttony, glad Nanette wasn't home, she wrapped the remaining part in its foil and slid it out of her immediate reach. As she did so, her hair splattered onto the tiled floor and despite the grief she knew to expect, she was pleased to feel it affixed to her head instead of severed and swept into piles in some trendy, faux-chic salon. As badly as she wanted a new look, she resigned herself for the time being to buying some new clothes instead. An entire spring wardrobe, if that was what it took. The Beethoven ended abruptly, seemingly in the middle of a waltz. The effect was jarring even before the CD changer rolled over to

Nan's most recent favorite band. It was noise, worse than static, and so popular that there was no getting away from it in any bar or supermarket. Melanie climbed out of the tub and wrapped her hair in a towel. She walked dripping through the apartment to change the music. It wasn't that she disliked pop music per se. Even Bartók incorporated many elements of the folk tradition into his works, and a generation of contemporary composers would inevitably do the same with hip-hop and techno, but even at its best, she considered this four-four nonsense somehow antithetical to the natural rhythms of the human body. Or at least to the natural rhythms of *her* body. Pop music demanded attention to its own carefully packaged and marketed angst, yet came nowhere close to the emotional depth of, say, String Quartet No. 6. That was about angst too, *real* angst: World War II, the demise of the composer's mother and motherland. The kind of music Melanie performed, or usually performed, had context. It had a spiritual depth. She put on Bartók's No. 6 and turned up the volume. Then she put down another towel and lay on the edge of the bed that she still, for some reason, shared with Nanette. Her toes touched the rug and her skin was warm and smooth from bathing. She was still holding the glass bottle of lotion. She felt good, loose. With her hangover gone, forgotten, she started to get dressed. The new clothes she had purchased for the occasion were splayed out like a snow angel on the bed, and they included her first-ever pair of thigh-high stockings. Ankle-length skirt, long-sleeve shirt, and flats. The concert memo specified that she wear all white. All wholly inappropriate before Easter, but white suited Melanie. The skirt fit wonderfully. She looked ravishing, or as close to ravishing as she could get. She put on a heavy, antique sterling choker handed down from her grandmother. Family legend had it that Paul Revere himself made the tiny ring that now served as the centerpiece. No earrings; her ears remained unpierced. No makeup—she couldn't stand how it felt on her skin.

She had just enough time to warm up. She played her scales, ran through some of the opera's trickier passages, and repacked her violin for the ride over to Batthyány Square. She would need to call a taxi. It was going to be a mob scene.

Most of Hungary's so-called Class of '56—those intellectuals who escaped during that year's brief anti-Soviet uprising—had come back for museum exhibitions, concert appearances, and every manner of artistic residency. Melanie had seen countless "living legends" of science and the humanities paraded down Andrássy Boulevard, past the opera house and Oktogon to Heroes' Square, where honor guards and cheering crowds welcomed them home. Hooray for Ernő Rubik and his cube! Harkályi had obviously left earlier, and in tragically different circumstances; his appearance today would mark his first trip to Hungary in decades, his first since he became an international sensation. The government had apparently tried to lure him back for years, since the success of his Symphony No. 4, and he had finally accepted the invitation. He had his pick of any concert hall and any orchestra in the world for the premiere of *The Golden Lotus*. Why he chose Budapest after all these years, much less the Opera Orchestra, was unclear.

Harkályi's opera presented few real challenges, but the score did require half of the violinists, including Melanie, to tune their instruments a quarter tone lower. The resulting dissonance could be startling both for an uninitiated audience and for those in the orchestra. Keeping up required a lot more concentration than did their usual repertoire. She suspected that this stylistic device derived subconsciously from his time at Terezín. During the formative stages of his development as a composer, he must have grown accustomed to the tones of rickety instruments and so he based much of his subsequent work on some uniquely personal timbral system emanating from his inner ear. She wasn't positive that was what had happened, but the theory went a long way toward her understanding of Harkályi's artistic voice. Maybe that was one reason she didn't hate this piece quite as much as she thought she would. And one section in particular, in the opera's waning minutes, truly excited her. At the conclusion of every concert there existed that brief moment when the music had stopped yet the conductor maintained a beat or two of silence before dropping his shoulders or in some way motioning to the audience that they could applaud. Nothing in Harkályi's oeuvre better lived up to the famous dictum about accounting for the "space between the notes," or in this case, *after* the notes. Instead of resolving with the big dominant-to-tonic chords loved so well by the Beethovens and Brahmses of this world, the entire orchestra and the four voices performed *around* the themes woven in during the first few acts. Those melodies existed, but only as negative space in the music. They were what was absent. Harkályi required his musicians to play in long, glassy circles of harmony, with the occasional quarter-tone flourish appearing underneath the veneer like cracks in a frozen pond.

At the end of the final scene, the instruments, and eventually the singers, would drop out one by one over the span of twelve minutes, until only a timpani and a traditional string quartet remained, just a hair out of tune, to saw over a folk-influenced section that vacillated between a funeral march and a spirited danse macabre, then close with a gentle lullaby. The opera didn't end as much as slowly, painfully die.

Melanie's violin, hidden in the rear of the section, would be the second-to-last thing the audience heard before the drums petered out into oblivion and presumably left the crowd enraptured and uncertain. She had been made to understand that she was chosen for the part not due to her abilities, but because her expensive Austrian violin possessed the perfect tone the part required. But so what? That breathless instant of tranquility right before the applause came would justify the endless rehearsals, the harassment and belittlement at the hands of that

Napoleon-complexed conductor. Even Melanie had to give Harkályi some credit—the effect was numbing in its gracefulness. At least that was how it had sounded at rehearsal.

5.

The taxi crossed Margit Bridge into Buda but couldn't get anywhere near Batthyány Square. The speakers immediately behind Melanie's head rattled with a warped cassette of frenetic Gypsy music, puking up tones no violin should ever be forced to make. The driver pulled to a stop at a makeshift police barricade and lit a cigarette. The stink competed with three pine-tree air fresheners dangling from the rearview mirror. Melanie felt vaguely queasy again. Two bored motorcycle cops in jackets of blue and white leather redirected traffic. The taxi driver rolled down his window for an explanation and a blast of cold air. More resigned than satisfied, the driver punched the meter and turned around with a ticket for 2,500 forints. Melanie handed him a five-thousand, but he shook his head. "No change," he said. He opened his leather accordion wallet to demonstrate the vast empty vistas contained therein—a common enough ploy among Budapest cabbies. At one time she would've let him take the fiver. Instead, she fished out a half dozen hundred-forint coins and handed them over. "Köszönöm szépen," she said sweetly, and stepped out into the cold. She half-expected him to get out and chase her down, but the bleating music faded behind her.

Her breath looked like cigar smoke, which was also approximately how her clothes smelled. She was five blocks from the concert site and already running late. Wooden, blue-painted barriers blocked the streets, strangely free of the parked cars that typically clogged the sidewalks. A precaution, she surmised, intended to protect the political dignitaries who would be attending the opera. The police had shut down the entire neighborhood, and pairs of patrolmen stood around smoking and cursing on every corner.

They never asked for her papírok. Unlike the majority of the expats she knew, Melanie's documents were both legit and legal.

Batthyány Square was a small city block–sized park across the Danube from the parliament building. Bums and drunks typically overran the benches and the subterranean red line metro station, secured for the afternoon, and would do so again once the camera crews and suits dispersed back up to the hills. Canapé tents and banks of lights filled the square, around which a fleet of shiny black Mercedes formed a double-parked ring. Many boasted diplomatic plates and ambassadorial flags.

On the southern end of the square stood a Baroque-era church, freshly painted for the occasion. Some accounts said that Beethoven personally conducted the premiere of his König Stephen overture in there, which, according to one historian, explained how the building survived two World Wars and the Soviet occupation. Melanie was in awe, nervous as all hell, again, at the prospect of personally meeting the spirit of Ludwig van Beethoven. And Mahler had once conducted for a season in the opera house, and that enlivened for her, at least slightly, even the most tedious reruns of yet another Erkel opera. She would sit in the pit and watch their little bastard of a conductor swirl his baton around and try to imagine old Gustav in the same position. Did his musicians, like they did nowadays, roll their eyes and make monkey ears behind his back? She imagined so. But Beethoven! The anticipation of performing in a church in which Beethoven himself brought to life those otherworldly notes and rests felt akin to walking in the footsteps of some true messiah. The promise of literal inspiration compelled her to get inside, to get in tune—and then correctly out of tune again. Because the recording engineers and the Hungarian secret service had occupied the church for the past week, the orchestra was never given the opportunity to rehearse there. She didn't know what to expect from the acoustics, from the aura.

A red carpet ran from the small fountain at the center of the square, across a street that was usually blocked by a line of pollution-spewing BKV buses, and down three steps into the church. The blinding-white exterior jumped out in extreme contrast to the dingy Angelika kávéház next door and, to the right of the square, the decaying redbrick railway station now owned by an Austrian supermarket conglomerate. A few soldiers milled around, guns drawn, sipping from Styrofoam cups of coffee, or something stronger. Portable outdoor heaters contributed to the overall merriment of the event.

According to the gossip filtering through the pit during rehearsals, the archbishop of Esztergom-Budapest had offered the orchestra the use of this church only after a three-part exposé in *HVG* elaborated the extent to which the Hungarian Catholic Church had collaborated with the Nazis. His eminence was expected to attend the premiere and, from the look of the security arrangements, so were the prime minister and perhaps even the president. Given the Hebraic flavor of Harkályi's oeuvre, no one of authority had seriously considered the national cathedral up on Castle Hill or even Saint Stephen's Basilica for the event.

Melanie's security clearance was going to depend upon her ability to find the orchestra's stage manager. That the party outside continued unabated provided a reason to stop worrying about being late. The sight of the freely flowing alcohol brought flashbacks to the night before, to the taste of the vodka no doubt continuing its path through her bloodstream. She was sweating under her collar when she heard someone call her name: "Melanie, hey!"

Woozy and distracted as she was, it actually came as an incredible relief to see Nanette, who gave her a sloppy public kiss. "You're here?"

"The prime minister's here, or coming here, so I got sent over. You didn't think I'd really miss your television debut? I wanted to surprise you. Here, I got it all scoped out." She was visibly drunk. She took

Melanie by the hand and led her through the celebrating throngs. "Sign in and you get an ID card. The security's tight."

"I didn't get my haircut."

"I fucking knew you wouldn't, but I'm glad."

"You're not going to give me grief about it?"

Nanette squeezed her hand. "I might, but not today. You can't take your phone backstage. I can drop it in my bag. If those metal detectors fuck up my film, I'm gonna kill someone. I guess I shouldn't say that so loud around here."

Poised between the intense Hungarian winter and the artificial suns alighting the square, between her childhood and her adult life, between her unrequited wanderlust and her blossoming desire to get back to Boston, Melanie remembered why she once loved Nanette so much, however briefly.

Nan brought her around the church and down Fő Street, which was also devoid of motor traffic and emptied of parked cars. A tree of intensely bright lights blocked the road and shone upon the modest, recently Windexed stained glass. Beyond the church they found a kind of truck trailer with a ticket window built into the side. A well-dressed will-call line snaked down the block, but Melanie stepped up to the window marked "Zenészek" and showed them her papers. A man in an Eskimo hood and mittens checked his clipboarded list and reluctantly handed her a photo ID badge to wear around her neck with instructions to remove it only once she got seated onstage. It was a terrible, living-dead picture, one of four taken in a Nyugati Station photo booth. He also gave her a ribbon of red, white, and green and ordered her to pin it over her heart.

Fucking foreigner, his eyes said to her.

"I should go," she said. Nanette gave her another drunken hug and Melanie joined the security line forming in the alley behind the church, where most of the brass section and even the woodwinds, whose instruments were in danger of cracking from the cold air, were required to prostrate their cases on the frigid cobblestones. They took apart and reassembled trumpets and flutes, played stray notes here and there for the benefit of the humorless secret service agents and mustachioed policemen. They ran her violin through a portable X-ray machine, then, cleared, she stepped through what passed for a stage door leading to a foyer behind the altar. Another sentry eyed her badge and without warning patted her forehead, cheeks, and nose with makeup powder intended, she supposed, to make her less shiny for the cameras. A card table along one wall had cups of mineral water and cold black coffee. Teenaged altar boys carried the musicians' coats and pocketbooks and instrument cases somewhere into the pit of the rectory and issued claim tickets that, instead of numbers, featured biblical verses. Melanie got one that said, "Nay, in all these things we are more than conquerors through him that loved us."

They used a cramped hallway as a kind of green room, from which she poked her head out into the church to get a feel for the space—far larger than it appeared from the outside—and to see about channeling the blessèd spirit of Beethoven. She strolled the perimeter of the room, climbed the conductor's riser. She felt disoriented, overwhelmed, anxious to get started.

There was no stage, no curtain. The altar had been carted off and their music stands and the rigid folding chairs sat splayed across the sanctuary, along with a dozen superfluous chairs that would go unused. The score to Harkályi's Symphony No. 4 included instructions for the orchestra to place extra, empty chairs amid the musicians on stage in order to "honor those souls freed from the earthly bonds of Auschwitz," and now organizers did the same thing at every concert of his music, whatever the composition. The stage crew today had placed empty chairs on the stage even though *The Golden Lotus* had absolutely nothing to do with the Holocaust. Quite a gimmick, but audiences loved it. Even with that extra spacing, the musicians would be playing right on top of each other. She pitied the bassoons, soon to be seated in front of the long-armed trombonists, until realizing that she might not have access to her bowing arm's full range of motion. When the production moved to the opera house, it was conceivable that the musicians would have to contend with empty chairs in the pit, even though no one else could see them, as if it wasn't claustrophobic enough down there.

The lights set up in the street outside amplified the colors of the stained glass, which shone directly onto the thirty or so rows of pews in which dozens of musicians sat adjusting reeds, head joints, and pegs while the party continued out on Batthyány Square. The clarinetists made quacking noises that rose up to a balcony, where the photographers and cameramen battled for position.

A few of her fellow orchestra members had recording contracts with Hungaroton and many others released their own homemade CDs of standard-repertoire chamber music. Some were very good players technically, one or two better than Melanie, but for the most part they lacked *feel*. The orchestra consisted of the least musical musicians with which she ever had the displeasure of performing. A band of castoffs, has-beens, and never-will-be's. The other, big orchestra in Budapest recorded for a London-based label and biannually toured the United States or Asia. When someone like a Schiff or a Solti returned to Hungary, he worked with that ensemble over at the Liszt Academy. For guest musicians, the Opera Orchestra got second-rate pop stars and novelty acts. They performed on heavy metal ballads by Edda and other aging Hungarian rockers. Perhaps it was their status as second fiddle that caused the general malaise she sensed even while they prepared for what was arguably the biggest concert in the orchestra's history. Or maybe growing up in a culture with such a rich musical legacy led to the blasé, unimpressed attitude about Beethoven's presence in the very same building. Either way, no one else appeared to revel in the musical spirit clinging to every pillar and pew. "Ludwig Beethoven stood right here!" she wanted to shout. "Don't you people get it?"

The stage manager, a portly beast of a man in rimless glasses, ordered the musicians to take their seats and remove their ID badges for the duration of the performance. Secret service agents moved silently into position among the stations of the cross and someone pulled open the main doors to invite in the cold air and several hundred dignitaries and hangers-on. The floor stopped rumbling, the heater turned off so the microphones wouldn't pick up the vibration. The rows of pews, divided by a center aisle, filled up fast. The stained glass threw prismatic colors at the faces and starched shirts of the quickly assembling congregation. Tickets for the event ran in the 100,000-forint range and didn't include seat assignments, so tuxedoed gentlemen elbowed each other to get up front. Murmurs rippled through the crowd and orchestra as various celebrities and prominent members of parliament made themselves visible among the three reserved and cordoned-off rows closest to the musicians. Red, white, and green banners hung from the ceiling and swayed amid the commotion.

Melanie placed her violin and bow on her lap and shook the blood down into her fingers. Warm, stony reverb filled every corner, each one lit up for reasons of national security and national television. She couldn't see Nanette. She wished she had thought to use the W.C.

The audience took its place. The lights flickered and then dimmed as the prime minister and his bat-faced wife entered from a door Melanie had not noticed before. Slowly, uncertainly, people stood and applauded. Those in the orchestra tapped their feet or bumped their bows gently against their music stands. Melanie shared a stand with a fifty-year-old housewife named Zsuzsi who smelled like burned toast and hadn't shaved her legs since glasnost. Not a good look with white stockings. Zsuzsi swooned like a schoolgirl at the sight of the prime minister, and even Melanie had to admit that he was more handsome in person than on TV. The happy couple turned their backs to the orchestra and gave the room a cheesy photo-op wave. They genuflected and crossed themselves before sitting.

Once the clamor receded and people sat again, a young tuxedoed man stood from the audience and hollered a string of obscenities and declarations that Melanie couldn't completely understand. He shouted something unintelligible about "There is no freedom in Hungary" and "Where is our grand democracy?" The crowd was aghast. One man took a swing at him. The entire orchestra, all eighty-plus musicians, did what they could to conceal their laughter as the security guards dragged the protestor out and no doubt beat him to a gooey pulp right there on the red carpet. The P.M. stood and faced the crowd again with a shrug of his shoulders and that self-deprecating smile he surely had practiced intently in front of a mirror. Cameras flashed on the balcony like Chernobyl-sized lightning bugs.

Then Lajos Harkályi, the guest of honor, entered with a buxom date not all that much older than Melanie. She prayed it was his daughter. A feverish, temporary insanity overtook the crowd. They stomped their feet and hooted. They clapped in unison the way Hungarian audiences did when extremely excited or extremely drunk. Or both, as was likely the case today. Somewhere, recording engineers fumbled to adjust input levels. Harkályi was tall, far taller than Melanie had imagined. He wore a natty new-fashioned tuxedo jacket, no tie. His nest of silver wooly hair was cut uncharacteristically close and neat for the occasion, compared to the style Melanie had seen in photos of him; his date sparkled with stage lights and sequins and the holy pseudo-virginal radiance of the stained glass. The prime minister hugged Harkályi. The composer and his girlfriend slid into the front-row pew, which had a block of empty seats reserved for the archbishop and president, who didn't show: more empty chairs.

The March weather seeped deeper into Melanie's fingers as the church grew colder. She hoped that the mass of people would soon generate some body heat, even if it was the odorous variety she knew to expect on the metro. The concertmaster—or kapo, as they called him—took the stage, his shoes click-clacking across the floor like a tap dancer's. Applause. He pointed to the principal oboe, who played a long A with which they all joined in to tune their instruments. Or un-tune them. Melanie was pleased with her tone and with the acoustics of the room. The kapo sat and noisily adjusted his chair until the conductor bounded in from off-stage. He climbed the podium to wild applause. Melanie would have liked to insert her violin bow into his rectum. The public didn't realize that this jerk's career leading an orchestra began only after he failed to demonstrate any affinity at all for composition, the violin, or even the piano—the instrument that made his mother famous throughout Europe after the war. Her name alone landed him and his older brother positions of tremendous importance within the hermetically sealed world of Hungary's musical establishment. Tellingly, no other orchestra had even considered him for as much as an assistant music directorship before now. His awkward, constipated-orangutan style and horrendously flawed ear annoyed Melanie to no end.

He stiffened his back and with a mild frown looked them over without making eye contact. He did nothing to establish a rapport with his orchestra. Nothing. They were strangers to him, despite the countless hours spent following his orders. A gesture as simple as a smile or even a nod would have put them—or at least it would have put *her*—squarely on his side. Instead, he adopted an adversarial posture. That thin sneer communicated something to the effect of, "Don't you dare fuck up the most important concert of my stillborn career." He raised his baton to begin the national anthem.

Ferenc Erkel's slow, plodding dirge was easily the world's most depressing hymn of self-celebration. The orchestra came in unevenly, so several of the violins rushed to find their spots. Every musician made mistakes on stage from time to time; the correct thing to do in most instances was to skip a few measures and follow along with the sheet music, with eyes only, until finding one's place and jumping back in. That these guys decided to play all the notes faster as a way of catching up to the rest of the orchestra only illustrated Melanie's concern about the level of amateurism she contended with every day at rehearsal. They played faster, but that only made the discord more apparent. If the audience noticed the initial gaffe, it didn't let on. Their esteemed conductor, however, grew visibly agitated. The music fell out of skew. Everything wobbled, unsure, for what felt like an hour. A train wreck was imminent. Panic grabbed hold of the reeds, who started to play faster to match the errant violins, until finally the timpanist took control of the situation—a responsibility that should have fallen squarely on the shoulders of the man with the baton—and leaned in a bit harder to establish a beat by which they could all correct themselves. It fell back into place just in time for the bleak finale. Melanie *felt* the music snap together more than heard it. From her seat she had a lousy view of the church and even, mercifully, of the conductor, but when they finally got into sync, the sonority of that room gave her chills. It was frigid to the point of disrespect for the musicians and audience, but the pinpricks up and down her arm derived not from the temperature, but from the immediately visceral sensation of hearing those gloriously melancholy tones reverberate through the eaves, of feeling Beethoven beside her. Within her. Locking in with other players, with a receptive audience, it was absolute joy. She even loved the usually tedious counting and keeping of time between her parts.

The applause hit them, a hot shower of jubilation and nationalistic pride. The conductor glowered, and then turned to the cheering crowd with the same thin smile. When he bowed in gratitude, his back to the orchestra, one of the tuba players cut loose with a sharp oompah. The sound was unmistakable. The tubist pretended it was an accident, that she was clearing the spit valve and it went off in her hands. The orchestra members couldn't reign in their laughter, their relief. That noise had unified them in direct opposition to their conductor. They staged a musical revolt, on Independence Day no less, and the conductor could only watch, dumbstruck as he lost his tenuous grip on an insolent ensemble. The tubist would certainly be fired. No question about it.

The raucous whooping and hollering wasn't simply the audience cheering the entrance of the soloists. It was that, but it was also the orchestra, up on the sanctuary where the altar should have been, laughing at something as inane and banal as a fart joke—a fart joke at the expense of their esteemed conductor. And that was where, less than a month later, the bestselling DVD recording of the event would begin. With this rambunctious laughter. With the conductor's face glowing bright pink in rage. With a shot of audience members who were unaware of what they had just witnessed and of what they were about to witness.

6.

The three soloists strutted out, unaware, into a musical minefield: soprano Erzsébet Holló, mezzo-soprano Judit Szirmay, and contralto Sylvia Péntek. Their dresses glittered, respectively, green, white, and red. Tenor László Nógrádi, the chansonnier, followed behind. The crowd erupted even more. The conductor, overcome with game-show host conviviality, lasciviously kissed the ladies and pumped Nógrádi's hand. Without room for sets, which were still under construction anyway, or for proper dressing rooms for costume changes, they performed a concert version of the opera. The singers sat at the front of the stage, facing the audience, except for Nógrádi, who remained standing.

Set in rural mainland China, *The Golden Lotus* used the practice of foot binding as a metaphor for the experience of the common man under what Harkályi described in the score's endnotes as the "corrupting sway and influence of capital." It had taken him thirty years to complete. He derived the title from the ideal shape that a woman's feet could attain by binding. According to the program notes, the wrapping of a young girl's feet—which typically started at age three or four—upheld patriarchic, feudal-era ideas of beauty. Small feet represented nobility even among peasants and raised one's social stature and prospects of good marriage. A mother would use a twenty-foot-long ribbon to adhere her daughter's toes to the underside of the foot, often crushing the bones in the process. She then sewed the ribbon ends together to prevent loosening and crammed the child's feet into shoes sometimes no more than a few inches long. As the flesh deteriorated, over time the stench of blood and pus could become overwhelming. When the bandages were drenched, the mother would scrape away the putrid flesh, tighten the ribbons further, and subject the girl to smaller and smaller shoes. The process lasted up to three years. The libretto described the sensation as something like walking through a fire. Harkályi, from what Melanie had read, also intended it as a jab at American decadence. Apparently the obsession with wealth and status not only hamstrung the nation's natural spiritual growth, but also brutally disfigured Americans in the process.

Nógrádi's spoken, chant-like introduction, which was in German, warned the audience and television cameras of the horrendous events they were about to witness, of the bondage to which people were subjected to in the name of beauty. In a remote Chinese village, Mother (Szirmay) defied her family, particularly Grandmother (Péntek), by refusing to bind the feet of her own infant Daughter (Holló). Mother and Daughter became objects of public scorn. Their shame cast an impenetrable shadow over the family's fortunes. After a minute and a half, a solo cimbalom came in to accompany Nógrádi. It evoked the timbre of a pipa. A strain of Asian music ran throughout the entire piece, but it carried a distinctly Magyar tone. The cimbalom remained a fixture of every Hungarian folk music ensemble and the associations with the local Gypsy music were unmistakable to the native audience.

Years had passed in the opera when the singing began in earnest. Nógrádi sat. This time, the orchestra came in together and the sound was staggering. They were one seamless mass: the orchestra and conductor and composer, the crowd and the cameras, the church and the city around them. The palpable spirit of Beethoven. Melanie felt it. The first part sung was the crying and moaning of the Daughter, now nine years old. Her big, unbound "peasant's feet" made her a pariah. As the strings assembled into shifting vistas of harmony, Daughter—with the help of Grandmother—bound her own feet in secret. It was an incredibly demanding part for a singer, full of abrupt transitions from precise lyricism to howls of physical agony and emotional duress. From her seat, Melanie saw the green-black of the singer's glittering gown, but little else.

Every musician was now on board and in precise and undistracted synchronization. The singers unfolded their story of pain and humiliation and violence wielded in the name of motherly love. Music surged in and out of tune. Harmonies arose and dissipated like clouds, then reformed themselves as hail that landed on the timpanis. The conductor smiled. His swaying grew more pronounced, more dance-like. Soon there were no longer notes on the page, only living music: music that consumed those black dots and rests like match heads and sent the ashes spewing all the way to the eaves, finally settling on the shoulders of prime ministers and diplomats and cameramen and Nanette somewhere firing away at Melanie through a zoom lens. A woman wailed, another sang solemnly, and yet another sat silent and motionless. Oboes and bassoons colored the very air they breathed and in which Melanie could now see her own breath. Horns blasted holes clear through the sound. The basses creaked and moaned like floorboards and the drums flagellated themselves mercilessly over her left shoulder to punctuate the entire event. Melanie watched her bow repeatedly stretch itself out from her body and recline again, hitting against the neck as if it were a talking drum. Her fingers danced heavily on the ridged strings, the bottom rim of her violin gouged into her collarbone, but she felt nothing. She possessed no "I" capable of feeling, and from that absence she was reborn into some kind of vision.

Melanie's body remained anchored to her chair—she never completely lost touch with her physical presence, yet a different part of herself became unmoored. Some kind of dream-self came removed from her body and hovered near the stage. She looked at herself there—*here*—playing the violin, and then she floated over the heads of the crowd and ventured through the front doors of the church. She followed the path of the river north to Margit Bridge and went down to the island, an oasis of groves and fields and footpaths. She sped over the tops of the trees. Colors appeared exceptionally vivid, yet somehow misaligned, like she was wearing a pair of wine-red lenses. She arrived at an enormous oak, one she had never seen before, and recognized it somehow as her home. She *belonged* in it. She joined a flock of eagles and hawks amid the branches, which elsewhere also contained bats and owls and pelicans and parrots of every color. It was the woodpeckers, however, that got her attention. Hundreds of them—woodpeckers of every variety, tap-tapping an intricate tribal rhythm. It was mesmerizing. The immediate sense of comfort overwhelmed her, like the familiarity of her own clean bed after a long trip. The voice of her violin joined the choral din of birdsong and roused her from her trance. Looking down, she nearly screamed, shaken not by the height, though she sat far higher than the top of any natural tree, but by a series of human bodies: black men dangled from the branches on ropes. They had been lynched and left to feed the amassed birds. The tops of their heads bobbed and swung heavily. Their dying moans sounded like upright basses and antique cellos tuned to some ungodly foreign scale. They accused Melanie of complicity. She fled back to Batthyány Square as the string quartet finale approached, much too suddenly. She was going to be late for her entrance. Daughter was dying from a painful gangrenous infection.

She tuned her pegs down by another quarter tone as required—but she didn't stop there. Instead, Melanie threw the strings wholly out of whack, even compared to the other atonal elements of Harkályi's precious composition, and deviated wildly from the score. Zsuzsi stirred in her seat but didn't risk looking over and losing her place; when her part ended and she stopped playing, the pronounced pocket of silence made Melanie's violin that much louder, more jarring. It sounded beautiful, alive and natural in a way that she could only think of as sexual. The first violins in front of her began to rock in their seats, visibly distraught. The conductor eyed her entire section, trying to identify the offending party. More instruments grew hushed on cue, like confused voices silencing themselves. The singers retook their seats. Melanie ignored the score in front of her. The cello and viola died slowly until only the timpani and her own screeching violin remained, as out of tune as an upright, elementary-school piano. Disbelief passed through the orchestra, followed by something like anger—now directed fully at her—but her bow kept seesawing away. She looked for the timpanist but couldn't see him. He struggled to keep up, to vamp along with Melanie and cover up the disaster in progress, but the combined effect soon breached that thin membrane separating music and noise. It sounded sirenlike, as natural as childbirth and just as messy. Even after the timpanist gave up, Melanie continued to play solo, exorcising herself of demons real and imagined. Filthy, infected sounds gushed from her body and every tone she dragged from her violin and ragged bow purged her of another sin until, at long last, she slid to one long, breathless glissando, then stopped.

The final altissimo squeak rose from the sounding board of her instrument, carried itself aloft, and ascended until it found itself trapped and muted among the plaster balusters of the ceiling. Calluses pulsated on her fingertips. The conductor eyed her in disbelief, in rage. He held his empty hand in front of his face as if shaking an invisible snow globe, then dropped it at his side before she was able to breathe again.

The church exploded. The audience's ecstasy found expression in the whistling and clapping and stomping of leather soles. The crowd jumped to its feet. The prime minister kissed his wife, shook the hands of well-wishers in the row behind him, and applauded with gusto. Melanie didn't dare to look at Harkályi. Her bow, a knot of horsehair tied to a stick, fell from her hand. The violinists in front of her turned around to stare without shame. The conductor took a jaunty bow and trotted off to the chancel. Beneath Melanie's feet the heaters mercifully—miraculously—came back to life.

The cacophony of shouts and applause solidified into a steady rollicking beat until the conductor took the stage again. Motioning to Harkályi, he held out his cupped palms the way a beggar might ask for spare change. Melanie braced herself. Lajos Harkályi stood, aglow with the triumph spilling down on him from the very walls of the church. Nothing about his composure, his countenance, gave the slightest hint of disapproval, yet Melanie's only concern involved collecting her things from those altar boys and getting the hell out before bumping into him. She didn't care about that wormy conductor, but she couldn't face Harkályi, not after the damage she had done to his opera. The prime minister hugged him and mugged for the cameras. The conductor pointed to the singers, asking them to stand. Bouquets fell at their feet. Erzsébet Holló received the loudest ovation and deservedly so. Her performance would make her a household name throughout Hungary and beyond.

The conductor waved his hand, directing those musicians who had distinguished themselves before his eyes to stand. He never took his gaze off Melanie but, needless to say, didn't lift her from her seat. Her career in Hungary was over. But a change came over the audience, a kind of clucking disapproval. Waves of protest rippled through the pews. Men pointed at her. The conductor, in his confusion, looked at Harkályi.

Melanie could see the composer's warm smile. He closed his eyes and nodded in what looked like acceptance, even joy. The conductor turned. He held his hand out toward her, and she stood. Tears streaked down her cheeks. Zsuzsi looked on in utter astonishment. The roar grew exponentially. Then the whole audience was standing. People cheered, yelled, clapped at her. Cameras in the balcony twinkled like distant, long-dead suns. Nanette stood behind one of them. Harkályi bounded up to the podium, raised the conductor's hand in triumph. The entire orchestra stood. Cameras continued to flash amid the cheers and a spontaneous eruption of a nationalistic hymn by the audience, after which they dispersed into their warm limousines.

The stage crew started to give the priests their church back, but Melanie remained in her seat. She wanted to run but had no place to go. She struggled to understand what had just happened. In that hallucination—if it *was* a hallucination—she could see herself clearly, as if standing somewhere beyond her embodied self. What she had experienced was real in the same way that she knew that her dreams were real, and the vision referred to her existence in the universe in the same way that her dreams spoke about her waking life. Strangely absent, however, was the gleeful ego rub that usually accompanied being the center of attention, getting singled out and applauded by an enthusiastic crowd. For the first time, she truly didn't care what the conductor or her fellow musicians or the audience had thought.

At one time, before that day, Melanie had considered her violin a part of her body, an appendage. But the music she, they, had just produced existed separately. It was now outside of her, beyond herself, and set loose into the wild to fend for itself on this bitterly cold March afternoon. That music no longer belonged to her any more than it belonged to Harkályi or to the conductor or to the audience. It was free. And so was she. Her informal resignation from the Opera House Symphony Orchestra had already been accepted, and she felt great about it. She felt liberated, her violin separate now, no longer hers. No one could possess such a thing. It was Independence Day. She sat amid the chaos of the altar's reconstruction and laughed until tears beaded in the corners of her eyes and a heavily accented voice addressed her. "I understand that you are an American?"

Lajos Harkályi pulled an empty chair over to face hers, scraping it across the stone floor. Behind him, the stained-glass window blinked out and the colors of the church faded back to their natural stony gray. Yet Harkályi's eyes still appeared bright, alive. Musical. An entourage of orchestra representatives and autograph seekers remained, for now, a respectful distance away. A reporter with a tape recorder cornered Harkályi's girlfriend.

Melanie wanted to apologize, but he cut her off.

"Do not be sorry," he said. "I have no problem with what has occurred today. What is your name?"

"Melanie Scholes."

"I am pleased to meet you, Melanie. I am Lajos."

She shook his hand, which was warm enough to bring the feeling flooding back to her fingers and toes. "I . . . I'm sorry I ruined the recording. Your premiere."

Nanette appeared among the clutter of stagehands and altar boys. Melanie shot her a give-me-a-sec look over Harkályi's shoulder. She snapped off a couple photos of the two of them, and it occurred to Melanie that she didn't need to *act* natural this time.

"On the contrary, I think that you may have saved it. I am flattered that my music moved you in such a way. It shows me that perhaps I did something correctly, and that you—" He yawned into the back of his hand. "Forgive me, I am extremely tired. It tells me that you have real music inside of you." Reporters clamored for his attention. "This is something we can discuss on another day." He pulled his billfold and a rotund ballpoint pen from the inner pocket of his jacket. "Here is my telephone number at home in Philadelphia. I will be there before the end of this month. Call me—collect, if that is what you prefer." He had the borderline-illegible handwriting of a child, but the surface of his business card was as smooth as marble. She tucked it between the strings of her violin. She stood when Harkályi did, and he hugged her in front of all those people, a public gesture of support. More cameras whirred and flashed at them. She got it, finally: Harkályi's popularity and subsequent wealth had rendered him invisible. But she now saw him, the real him, or at least believed that she did. In becoming an icon he had sacrificed his complexity, the fluid motion of his humanity. And it seemed like he had accepted that, made his peace with it. Of his millions of fans, Melanie alone knew him, understood who he was. She held him tighter. The shoulder of his luxuriously soft jacket absorbed her tears before he was swallowed up by his followers and devotees.

7.

Nanette threw her arms around Melanie's neck. "Baby, you were great!" she screamed. "That was so cool. What did the composer guy say?"

Confusion impeded Melanie's attempt at a rational response. She didn't want to talk about it, least of all with Nanette. No words existed in English or Hungarian for what she had experienced. For what she was still experiencing. Music she had never heard before appeared in her head. She needed to write it down.

The vision, or whatever it was, wouldn't fade. It embedded itself in her mind like a catchy melody. It defied meaning. She realized something crucial, however: it was time to go. She needed to leave Budapest, to leave Nanette, and to return to the comfort she had found up in that impossibly tall tree, until the lynched chorus began to holler. Something in that brief, initial sensation of serenity triggered an acute understanding of how miserable she was with the recklessness, with the out-all-night bacchanalia she used to distract herself for a few hours at a time from the music she felt surging through her veins. Something in the horror of seeing those men dangling, hearing their moans, which would continue to haunt her for years to come, told Melanie that she had lost all sight of what made her who she was.

She didn't want to blame Nanette, however: she bore full responsibility herself, which was why she needed to leave Budapest and her expatriate life behind. On a practical level, she was likely out of a job anyway. No way the conductor would have her back. She had contemplated the move for ages, even checking ticket prices and looking at audition dates with orchestras in Philly and Baltimore, Washington and Boston, but had always hesitated to give up the privilege of the expatriate lifestyle. Here, she was an American. Back in the States, she would become just another aimless kid with a violin, like all the other conservatory dropouts working in music stores and performing for community theater. But this concert sealed the deal. Leaving was no longer an option—it was a necessity. She was trapped. If she had to, she would move in with her brother and his wife for a few weeks. Take on some private students and practice her butt off until the next round of Boston Symphony auditions.

"Did you get a program?" she asked Nanette.

"Yeah, here." Nanette fished a copy from the side pocket of a camera bag.

There was little room to write amid the program notes and biographical information and the colorful advertisements for Unicum, salami, and banks. "Give me a pen."

"What—?"

"Hold on," Melanie said, and jotted down the first few notes of a simple melody, a theme. She heard it over and over, like a skipping record.

More would come soon. She felt it brewing inside her. She had never composed music before, and wasn't entirely sure that was what she was doing, but it seemed like it. The melody was both unrecognizable and as familiar as her own name. She handed the pen back to Nanette.

"What did the composer say?"

Melanie would wait until later to tell Nanette that she was leaving. "He . . . he thanked me."

"Isn't he really famous?"

"Let me get my stuff and we'll go."

Nanette sat and held Melanie's violin and bow in her lap. Melanie pocketed Harkályi's business card and exchanged her Bible verse for her case and coat. The conductor, speaking into a Magyar Televízió microphone, gave her a look of pure evil that would make the front page of the next day's *Hírlap*. Back on stage, Melanie wiped down the strings and placed her instrument into its snug little coffin. Nanette put her arm around her shoulders, and on their way out the church doors Melanie offered a silent prayer of thanks to Beethoven. He heard her. He was grateful too.

Nanette called for a taxi. The shivers running through Melanie's spine had nothing to do with the weather.

"Get a beer?" Nanette asked, of course.

The idea didn't appeal in the slightest, but Melanie liked the idea of finding some neutral ground to tell Nanette her plans. She didn't want to be back in that gross apartment, unless it was to book the soonest possible flight home.

"I want to change first. Get out of these shoes. Meet you down there?"

"Baby, it's on me tonight."

"Totally unnecessary. I'm thrilled you made it."

"And miss your superstar debut? Fat chance. What else did Harkaly say to you?" His mispronounced name sounded strange on Nanette's lips, almost indecent.

"Harkályi. He said he liked my playing. That I should call him."

"That is so cool."

Melanie's reflection shone in the taxi's window. The dome of the parliament building was lit up. "You have no idea."

The taxi stopped halfway across Margit Bridge, the traffic around it frozen into a solid brick of metal and engine noise, carbon monoxide, and car horns. It would be faster to walk home. Nanette handed the driver some cash, and they spilled out onto the sidewalk. Cold as it was, they stopped at the same observation deck they had visited late the previous night. This morning. No view of Budapest was more spectacular. Nanette stood behind Melanie and put her arms around her chest, pinning her arms to her body.

Melanie contemplated throwing her violin into the water, along with the case and the bow and everything else. A fresh start. The melody forming in her head stopped her. Though currently only eight measures long, it felt like it had been with her forever. As the sound multiplied, the notes didn't merely arrange themselves linearly into a longer composition. They also grew horizontally, starting with a lone violin, her own, which was joined by more instruments and more tone colors. She held fast to her music case and soon heard an entire string section and percussion—urgent tribal drumming, like a work song, like those woodpeckers—until now twelve measures of a spacious orchestral work repeated in her ears again and again. It was beautiful. She couldn't hear the entire symphony, not yet, but she *felt* what it would sound like. Amid the reflected lights, the river had a deep, lustrous blue color. The burst of music in her head was like an act of resistance, an antidote to the cold, most immediately, but also to Hungary. To the incestuous claustrophobia of expatriate life. To Nanette.

Melanie was humming to herself when Nan spun her around with a clanging of cameras and kissed her over and over on the lips. She was too rough.

"I'm leaving," Melanie told her.

"I know." Nanette had been crying too. She kissed Melanie again, even harder. Like she was angry. She was hurting her.

"I'm not leaving *you,"* Melanie said. It was a lie, and they both knew it. She heard the music more clearly than her own words. "I'm leaving Hungary. I have to get out of here."

"Baby, I fucking hate this city," Nanette said. "Let's go somewhere else. Let's go to Vienna, like you've been saying. You can't leave. That photo I want to shoot, the iconic one—I just have this *sense* somehow that you're going to be in it."

Maybe you've already taken it, Melanie wanted to say, but didn't. Leaving Budapest would be more difficult than she had hoped. "I'm going home," she said.

"What do you mean 'home?'" Nanette's voice sounded like a squealing oboe, the instrument the rest of an orchestra will use to get in tune.

"Back to Boston," Melanie said. She had work to do, work she could never accomplish living this way. She needed to call Harkályi.

Nanette wiped her running nose. "You can't leave me here."

Melanie stared at the water, taking in the view, with no interest in discussing what they both knew would happen next. She couldn't wait to get into comfier clothes, to get the mask of makeup powder off her skin. Unwilling to argue, she headed back toward the Coca-Cola sign. Nanette followed her part of the way, then went into Eve and Adam's to find a booth.

Melanie trudged up the stairs to their stinking, filthy apartment. So many steps. Her violin case swung at her side. She needed a change of clothes, and then to find Nan's good scissors. First, though, she really needed to transcribe in her neatest handwriting the series of notes that would soon make up the main theme of her Symphony No. 1 ("Duna").

EXTRAORDINARY RENDITIONS

COLOPHON

In honor of this book's Hungarian setting, the text has been set in Ehrhardt type, which was designed by Miklós (Nicholas) Kis. After taking religious orders, Kis traveled to Amsterdam in the late seventeenth century to learn the arts of printing, type design, punch cutting, and type casting. He not only learned these skills, he excelled, creating an amazing number of outstanding fonts during an estimated ten-year period. Then, as planned, he brought his new skills back to Hungary and printed several editions of the Bible and other religious books in the Hungarian language before his death in 1702 at the age of fifty-two. Perhaps it was because he was a humble, religious man, perhaps it was because he was a foreigner and was no longer around to claim credit, but whatever the reason, all of the fonts he created in Holland were initially attributed to other designers, including Janson and an extensive range of Greek and Hebrew fonts, in addition to Ehrhardt. Only within the second half of the twentieth century has the full range of his achievement been revealed by typographic historians. The full impact of his work on the development of Hungarian publishing and culture is still being evaluated. At Coffee House Press we lift our mug to salute the many unknown artists who contribute to our shared culture.

The coffee houses of seventeenth-century England were places of fellowship where ideas could be freely exchanged. In the cafés of Paris in the early years of the twentieth century, the surrealist, cubist, and dada art movements began. The coffee houses of 1950s America provided refuge and tremendous literary energy. Today, coffee house culture abounds at corner shops and online.

Coffee House Press continues these rich traditions. We envision all our authors and all our readers—be they in their living room chairs, at the beach, or in their beds—joining us around an ever-expandable table, drinking coffee and telling tales. And in the process of this exchange of stories by writers who speak from many communities and cultures, the American mosaic becomes reinvented, and reinvigorated.

We invite you to join us in our effort to welcome new readers to our table, and to the tales told in the pages of Coffee House Press books.

Please visit www.coffeehousepress.org
for more information.

FUNDER ACKNOWLEDGMENTS

Coffee House Press is an independent nonprofit literary publisher. Our books are made possible through the generous support of grants and gifts from many foundations, corporate giving programs, state and federal support, and through donations from individuals who believe in the transformational power of literature. Coffee House Press receives major operating support from the Bush Foundation, the McKnight Foundation, from Target, and from the Minnesota State Arts Board, through an appropriation from the Minnesota State Legislature and from the National Endowment for the Arts. Coffee House also receives support from: three anonymous donors; Abraham Associates; Allan Appel; Around Town Literary Media Guides; Bill Berkson; the James L. and Nancy J. Bildner Foundation; the Patrick and Aimee Butler Family Foundation; the Buuck Family Foundation; Dorsey & Whitney, LLP; Fredrikson & Byron, P.A.; Sally French; Jennifer Haugh; Anselm Hollo and Jane Dalrymple-Hollo; Jeffrey Hom; Stephen and Isabel Keating; Robert and Margaret Kinney; the Kenneth Koch Literary Estate; the Lenfestey Family Foundation; Ethan J. Litman; Mary McDermid; Sjur Midness and Briar Andresen; the Rehael Fund of the Minneapolis Foundation; Deborah Reynolds; Schwegman, Lundberg, Woessner, P.A.; John Sjoberg; David Smith; Charles Steffey and Suzannah Martin; Mary Strand and Tom Fraser; Jeffrey Sugerman; the Archie D. & Bertha H. Walker Foundation; Stu Wilson and Mel Barker; the Woessner Freeman Family Foundation in memory of David Hilton; and many other generous individual donors.

This activity is made possible in part by a grant from the Minnesota State Arts Board, through an appropriation by the Minnesota State Legislature and a grant from the National Endowment for the Arts.

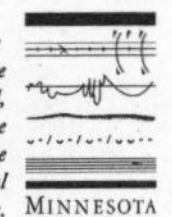

To you and our many readers across the country,
we send our thanks for your continuing support.